D1291054

JACK OF HEARTS

A DETECTIVE JACK STRATTON NOVEL

CHRISTOPHER GREYSON

GREYSON MEDIA

Novels featuring Jack Stratton in order:

AND THEN SHE WAS GONE
GIRL JACKED
JACK KNIFED
JACKS ARE WILD
JACK AND THE GIANT KILLER
DATA JACK
JACK OF HEARTS
JACK FROST

Also by Christopher Greyson:

PURE OF HEART

THE GIRL WHO LIVED

JACK OF HEARTS
Copyright © Greyson Media August 14, 2017

The right of Christopher Greyson to be identified as author of this Work has been asserted by him in accordance with sections 77 and 78 of the Copyright, Designs and Patents Act 1988.

All rights reserved. No part of this publication may be reproduced, distributed, or transmitted in any form or by any means, including photocopying, recording, or other electronic or mechanical methods, without the prior written permission of the publisher.

This book is licensed for your personal enjoyment only. This eBook may not be resold or given away to other people. If you would like to share this book with another person, please purchase an additional copy for each recipient. If you're reading this book and didn't purchase it, or it was not purchased for your use only, then please purchase your own copy. Thank you for respecting the hard work of this author.

Find out more about the author and upcoming books online at www.ChristopherGreyson.com.

ISBN: 1-68399-070-6
ISBN-13: 978-1-68399-070-3

This book is dedicated to my parents, Ted and Laura. Together briefly, but eternally united, their timeless love will always be an inspiration to me.

CONTENTS

Chapter 1 - A Good Thing Going 1
Chapter 2 - Pause the Game 7
Chapter 3 - Aviophobia 9
Chapter 4 - Rule Number One 13
Chapter 5 - Not My Idea 15
Chapter 6 - Beware of Alligators 24
Chapter 7 - I Love You, Lady 29
Chapter 8 - So You Got a Boo-Boo 34
Chapter 9 - A Fine-Looking Boy 36
Chapter 10 - Animal Control 39
Chapter 11 - Two by Four 42
Chapter 12 - The Battle Butterfly 46
Chapter 13 - A Bad Idea 49
Chapter 14 - I'd Like to Join 54
Chapter 15 - Jumping to Conclusions 57
Chapter 16 - No Pressure 61
Chapter 17 - Theories and Lists 64
Chapter 18 - Special Delivery 67
Chapter 19 - The Shadow Man 70
Chapter 20 - Give the Man a Cigar 74
Chapter 21 - A Singing Frog 77
Chapter 22 - What Happened to the Door? 80
Chapter 23 - Taken to the Cleaners 82
Chapter 24 - Digging 85
Chapter 25 - Bait 87
Chapter 26 - Look, I'm Invisible 93
Chapter 27 - My Home 96
Chapter 28 - Think Like a Criminal 98
Chapter 29 - Delay of Game 103
Chapter 30 - Leash the Beast 105
Chapter 31 - Loose Ends 108
Chapter 32 - Swamp Water from Hell 110
Chapter 33 - It Was a Good Plan 113
Chapter 34 - Surprise 116
Chapter 35 - Embrace the Hate 118
Chapter 36 - Old Friends 121
Chapter 37 - Love-struck 124
Chapter 38 - Let Him Sleep 126
Chapter 39 - In on It 128
Chapter 40 - That's Amore 130
Chapter 41 - Pedal to the Metal 132
Chapter 42 - Help or Get Out of My Way! 138
Chapter 43 - Benched 141
Chapter 44 - Promise 143

Chapter 45 - Chapel 144
Chapter 46 - You Owe Me..146
Chapter 47 - Tuna Casserole 149
Chapter 48 - Hanging with Goofy..151
The Detective Jack Stratton Mystery-Thriller Series..................................155
Acknowledgments 155
About the Author..161

1

A GOOD THING GOING

"Was the funeral fun?"

Leaning his tall frame against the lanai doors, Curtis Dixon held up the memorial service bulletin and chuckled at his own handiwork. The picture of the elderly woman's face on the front was now covered with glasses and a bushy mustache.

"You shouldn't have killed her." His aunt's words clicked as sharply as her high heels as she marched across the tiles of the grand living room and plucked the bulletin from his hand. The ice in her rum runner tapped against her glass when she stopped.

"She slipped getting into the bathtub," Dixon said. "It's not my fault if old people are clumsy." He shrugged, and his taut muscles rippled beneath tan skin.

"You were only supposed to pick up the package. We don't need this extra attention."

She was still dressed in her black business suit from the funeral, and every time Dixon saw her in that suit, he pictured her berating the cowering employees in the posh office in which she had once worked. How many times had she told him the stupid story of how she had risen from poverty to run one of the largest fashion magazines in the world? That was years ago and she'd long since retired, but how she loved to remind him of how powerful she'd once been.

Of course, Dixon knew *how* she'd risen from poverty. She had been a dancer in a strip club, along with Dixon's mother, when a rich old businessman had taken a fancy to her—and married her. And just like that, it was goodbye poverty, hello glitz and glamour. He eyed her slender frame. She was pushing seventy, but between the gym, plastic surgeons, and spa treatments, she was still a looker.

"Is that why you called me?" Dixon asked. Outside the glass doors, dozens of streetlights across the retirement community snapped on. "Just to rag at me about a dead old lady nobody is even going to miss?"

"I need you to pick up another package, Curtis. The address is 4 Gulf Coast. Roy McCord."

Dixon's eyes brightened like the streetlights. He inhaled through his nose and his chest swelled.

"Just get the package. There's one elderly man living there, and his bedroom is in the back-right corner of the house. *No one dies.* Is that clear?"

"Will you stop blaming me?" Dixon held out his arms, stretching the tattoos of cobras that wrapped around his thick forearms and twisted over his bulging biceps.

The snakes pointed to a tattooed Anubis with red eyes that covered his neck and disappeared into his black tank top.

Dixon's show of brawn had the desired effect. Fear tightened his aunt's face and the ice in her glass tinkled as her hand shook slightly.

"Old people die," he said. "Some of them slip down the stairs. Others fall asleep with a pillow on their face."

"Every time someone dies, they investigate," his aunt snapped. "Pick up the package tonight. Nothing more."

Dixon stepped so close to his aunt that they were almost cheek to cheek. But she'd had time to compose herself, and she was steady as she stared at him with blue eyes as cold as the ice in her tumbler.

"You have a good thing going here, Curtis. Don't blow it by killing anyone else."

Dixon kissed her cheek. "For you, Auntie, anything."

***

Roy McCord tossed back the blanket and rolled out of bed. He didn't bother turning on the light; his eyes were used to the dark, as he'd been staring at the ceiling for the past two hours. Ever since the nightmare had awoken him.

He glanced at the clock on the nightstand: 1:04 a.m.

He knew that he'd go back to sleep later tonight, but he made the bed just the same, pulling the blanket tight enough to bounce a quarter off the surface. *Old habits die hard.* He'd been out of the service for forty years, but once a marine, always a marine. He still wore his gray hair in a high and tight crew cut, and he carried himself with his shoulders back, chest out, and chin down.

He smoothed the top sheet and headed for the living room. The streetlights that dotted the retirement community provided enough glow for him to see. His eyesight hadn't gone south with him to Florida. He was grateful for that.

He looked out at the empty street and listened to the quiet. The silence had weight— a presence, even.

As he watched, the front door across the street opened, and Bernie Lane stomped out, tying his bathrobe, his gangly poodle in tow. They say people tend to look like their dogs, and Bernie was proof of that. His white hair shot out in all directions, as if he'd been electrocuted. If he put the dog on his head, you'd wonder where the dog went.

Bernie grumbled and griped at the dog while it did its business. Roy grinned as the dog kept changing its mind where it wanted to go. *I should get a dog.* He walked over to the corner cabinet. *A collie maybe.*

He poured himself a small glass of whiskey and headed for the recliner. He tried to relax into the soft chair, but his whole body was tense and sweaty. The air conditioning was on, but it couldn't keep up with this heat. Lately it had been pushing ninety-five, even at night.

"Maybe I should have moved to Montana," he muttered as he sipped his drink.

Roy glanced down at the wedding picture on the end table, but quickly looked away. It was getting close to their wedding anniversary. His Anne had been gone almost ten years now, but the glimpse of her pretty face made his chest tighten. He ached for her. Sometimes he still half-expected to hear her voice call to him from the other room; other times he wondered when she would get home, as if she had just gone out for a walk. Tonight, she would have walked into the living room, taken the drink from his hand, and brought him back to bed.

He took another bitter sip.

Their son was gone, too. Cancer took him five years prior. His daughter-in-law had remarried last year. They didn't have any kids, so Roy was alone. Even the guys in his squad were almost all gone. He only had one friend left. And now that Darius had stomach cancer…

He took a long sip.

At least he'd given Darius one last hurrah. He swirled his glass as he remembered their recent trip to the Bahamas. Glancing at the dolphin statue on the mantel, he chuckled. He had broken even at the casino, but they gave him a statue anyway. A silly thing, but to him it was a reminder of a good time with a friend.

Roy had won the trip for two at bingo, and he immediately knew he'd take Darius. Who else? Of course, at their age, it wasn't like old times. Back in the day, he and Darius would get thrown out of a bar at closing time; now they were in bed by ten. "Like a couple of little old ladies," Darius joked.

A laugh started to build, but it was cut off by Roy's tightening throat.

Thinking of Darius reminded him of the nightmare that had awoken him earlier. Not so much a nightmare as a memory. A memory of a nightmare.

The Battle of Huế.

It happened during that one month of sheer hell in Vietnam. A month that burned so hot he knew he'd never leave it behind. It had branded him for life.

It was during that month, during that battle, that the nightmare began. One hot night, the Vietcong had them pinned down in a tiny village. And from where they crouched, silently, Roy could see a wounded young American soldier lying out in the street. Everyone said the soldier was dead, but Roy wasn't certain. Every once in a while, Roy could have sworn that the soldier moved. Roy didn't know his name, didn't know how he'd ended up there, but as they hid in the dark, Roy couldn't help but watch him. For hours, he looked out at the man—a boy, really—and thought: *That could've been me.*

The young soldier lay on his side in front of what was probably once a pretty little flower garden. It was a six-foot square surrounded by a two-foot-high rock wall. In front of it was a stone bench. Roy could imagine the garden filled with spring flowers, but right now it was a barren patch of dirt.

The soldier must have been trying to dive into it for cover.

He never made it.

Seeing something like that changes a man. Hiding in the dark with the heat and quiet and turning your mind inward does something to you. Sometimes it's good. It makes you assess where you are and where you're going. Other times, it does something else to you.

Something not so good.

Around midnight, the soldier moved again. Roy's CO said it was rigor mortis setting in, but Roy knew it wasn't.

He took another sip of whiskey.

It could've been me.

Lying there like a hurt dog in the street.

Slowly dying.

With a crowd of people watching.

I'd want someone to get me the hell outta there.

As the night ticked slowly onward, the thought kept repeating in his head: *It could have been me... It could have been me.*

And then he added another thought to the mantra: *Treat others the same way you want them to treat you.* Since he was a little boy, his mother had drilled that philosophy into his head. It was sage advice, but not so easy to obey when following through on it might get your head blown off.

When the boy moved again, so did Roy. He crawled. He pressed his body as flat against the ground as he could and went slow. The street was littered with sharp gravel, blasted loose by explosives and gunfire. Every time he pulled himself forward, the scrape of the little rocks against the tar sounded like thunder in his ears.

It took several minutes to reach the soldier. They were the longest and worst minutes of his life. He felt like a condemned man standing before the firing squad, waiting for the bullets to rip him apart.

When he finally made it, the soldier's eyes fluttered open.

Blue. The color of a clear summer sky.

The kid didn't say anything, but gratitude shone in those blue eyes. Roy would never forget that. *How do you thank a guy for crawling into hell to get you?*

But any hope of getting them both out of there vanished in a hail of bullets. Metal rain poured down on the town square, turning night into day. Roy yanked the soldier under the stone bench and pulled them both against the rock-walled flower bed.

Metal shrieked as it shattered against the wall. Bullets pulverized the stone into clouds of dust. Rock fragments scattered like buckshot, tearing at their skin.

The Americans responded with a hellfire of their own.

Trapped between two massive firework displays, Roy felt wave after wave of sound ripple through his body. The stone shielded him and the soldier from most of the onslaught. But there was a small gap between the bench and the wall, less than an inch at most, and with so many bullets flying, an inch was too much.

One bullet made it through.

Roy looked down at his right hand. Next to the old battle scar was a fresh one on his knuckle.

He sipped the whiskey.

As Roy had aged, so had his bones; they were breaking down like the rest of him. For forty-five years, a piece of that bullet had remained lodged in his hand, until three months ago when it broke free. He woke up one morning with his hand looking like someone had blown up a rubber glove. It had swelled to double its normal size. The doctors removed the shrapnel, but his old hand ached more now than it ever had.

He received a Purple Heart for that one. He earned another when he got shot in the leg three months later. He was awarded a Bronze Star for rescuing the soldier.

Medals. Scars. Just different ways of remembering things you'd rather forget.

From somewhere in the rear of the house, a sound pulled Roy from his dark memories. A little suck of air, and then something sliding. For a second, he thought that Anne had opened the refrigerator, but that was impossible. Anne was gone. He was all alone.

Someone had opened a window.

Roy set his drink down on the end table without making a sound. He missed the coaster. He could hear Anne's voice warning him about leaving a ring on the wood. He almost whispered back, "Not now."

His heart pounded in his chest with deep thuds. He kept a baseball bat in the kitchen by the door, but that was too far to be of any use. *I really wish I'd gotten a dog.*

Another noise came from the back of the house. His heartbeat pulsed in his ears so loudly he could barely identify the sound.

Pantry door.

As Roy moved quietly to the wall, the whole room seemed to roll. He cursed when he saw his hand tremble. *Fool.* He steadied himself by holding onto the mantel.

A chair in the kitchen made the slightest scuff. Someone was making their way through Roy's house. They were coming closer now.

Roy looked for something he could use as a weapon, but there was nothing. He balled his hand into a fist.

One punch. I have to have at least one good one left in me.

Roy's temples throbbed. He inched closer to the kitchen door.

The door swung slowly open.

Roy felt as if he'd been shot in the chest with an arrow. Piercing pain radiated outward briefly and then raced down his left arm. It hurt to breathe.

Not now.

He groaned. The pain was so intense he dropped to his knees.

A man peered out from the kitchen. His hair was long and made his thin face look gaunt. The intruder stood frozen in the doorway and stared at the old marine on his knees.

"Take what you want and go," Roy gasped as he crawled to the phone.

The man lunged forward and cut Roy off. He stood with his feet planted and his shoulders squared, as if he were about to swing.

Roy shook his head. "Ambulance. Just go." The room spun, and Roy fell face-first to the floor.

The man wore sneakers and jeans. He set a small black backpack at his feet and crouched down in front of Roy. His eyes were a gray-blue, like a cold winter's day. He extended his heavily tattooed arms and tilted his head back, revealing a tattoo that looked like some Egyptian dog statue with red eyes.

"Welcome to death." A thin smile spread across the man's face as he gazed down at Roy.

Roy had seen that look before. Most men hated killing, but in war, some realized that the power to bring death was something they enjoyed. As the blue in the man's eyes brightened, Roy realized that tonight he was going to die.

The invisible bands squeezed Roy's chest harder. He felt as if an elephant were sitting on his chest. His square jaw tightened as the crushing pain intensified. What little strength he had left was slowly draining away.

The man opened the backpack and pulled out a white nylon rope. The rope was coiled except for the end, which was tied into a noose. The man held it up and let the noose swing back and forth.

Roy began to foam at the mouth.

"You gotta be kiddin' me, old man. Do you know how long it took me to tie this, and now you're gonna go and kick it with a heart attack?" The man huffed, stood, walked to the recliner, and sat. He reached out a gloved hand and picked up Roy's glass. "Tell you what, I'll give you a choice. You can lie there and die or," he wiggled the noose, "I'll help you out. You get to decide how you're going to die. Take your time." He stretched his legs out and took a sip. "But know this: if it takes you longer to croak than it takes me to finish this drink, you're going to decide to commit suicide."

Roy's hand twitched. He tried to slide his arm forward, but his body wasn't responding to his commands. He had never thought too much about how he'd die, but even in his worst nightmares he had never imagined he'd die like a dog on the floor while some punk sat on his recliner, drinking his whiskey.

"You were a soldier, huh?" The man picked up the photo of Roy and his wife. "She was hot! She's dead, right? Too bad. I've always wanted a two-fer."

Roy groaned. Pain wracked his chest as if a bat were repeatedly smacking his rib cage.

"Come on. Say something. Guys like you always want to hear themselves talk." The man took a long sip and then tapped the glass with a fingernail. "Past the halfway mark. Looks like we might have a hanging after all."

Roy stared at the man. "Why?" The question escaped Roy's mouth before he realized he didn't really want to know. *What could possess anyone to enjoy watching someone die?*

"Why a hanging?" The man put his feet on the floor and his elbows on his knees as if he were discussing a football game with a friend. "Because no one is going to think twice if an old guy says screw it, has a couple of drinks, and realizes that he has no purpose and should do the world a favor and get the hell off it." He tilted his head back, drained the glass, and slammed it down on the table. "But that's not what you were asking me, was it? I bet you're just like my grandfather. He was a soldier too. He looked at me the same way you are now. *He's* why." The man stood and wiped his mouth with the back of his hand. "I'm done with my drink." He stepped over Roy.

Roy watched the thief. Out of all of the things in the house, he reached out and picked up the last thing Roy would have guessed he'd steal.

"It was real fun hanging my grandfather and watching him dance," the man said. "His feet kicked a long time. His face turned a deep purple, and boy did he stare then. His eyes were almost popping out of his head. I wonder if that's what you're gonna do."

The man kept talking, but Roy didn't hear him anymore. His words sounded far away, and Roy was grateful to be fading out. He was almost dead anyway; there was nothing this man could do to him.

Just before his eyes closed for the last time, Roy couldn't help but wonder: *Why would he steal that?*

2

PAUSE THE GAME

THREE WEEKS LATER

Jack parked in front of the little ranch house, and the whole car rocked as his King Shepherd, Lady, stood up on the backseat and stretched. Jack reached back and scratched behind her ears. "This is the last stop. I promise."

He took out his notebook and reviewed the names listed on the page. All of them had been crossed out except for one: Amanda Muldoon.

Jack hurried across the street and knocked on the cranberry-red door. He ran a hand through his thick brown hair and smiled slightly. He was a handsome man, but at six foot one and a fit one hundred and ninety-five pounds, he could come off as intimidating. A few seconds later, the door opened an inch until it hit the chain still securing it. Wary brown eyes peered out.

"Ms. Strauss? I'm Jack Stratton. I called and left a message. I'm trying to find—"

"Hold on." The door shut, a chain rattled, and the door opened again. An older woman with auburn hair looked Jack up and down. "We bought the house from the Muldoons."

"Who's at the door?" a man called out from inside the house.

"That guy who called looking for the Muldoons. Will you pause the game? I want to watch it too."

Jack heard the roar of a sports crowd coming from the other room.

"I can't pause it," the man said.

"Why not?" the woman snapped.

"I can't find the remote!"

The woman glared at Jack. "I'm missing the game. What do you want?"

"I'll only be a minute. I'm trying to locate Amanda Muldoon. She was a friend of my girlfriend's mother, and—"

The crowd on the TV cheered.

"They just tied it up!" the man exclaimed.

The woman stamped her foot. "Like I said, we bought the house from them. We weren't friends or nothing. They moved. I don't know where." She started to shut the door, but Jack shot his foot forward to act as a doorstop.

"I'm sorry, but it's really important that I track Amanda down. Did she mention anything about where she was moving?"

The woman shrugged. "I don't know. It was ten years ago."

Footsteps sounded in the hallway behind the woman, and a man in a stained T-shirt, with an empty beer bottle in his hand, appeared. "Get rid of him," he whispered loudly enough for Jack to hear.

"Did you find the remote?" she asked.

"It's half-time."

The woman huffed at Jack.

"Look, I'm sorry to interrupt your game." Jack reached into his pocket and pulled out a twenty. "Get a pizza on me. I just need you to try to remember anything that can help me find Amanda. It's really important."

The woman's face scrunched up and she brought her hand up to her chin. "Wait there." She glanced at the man and tipped her head back to Jack before she walked away down the hall.

The man groaned. He lifted the beer bottle to his lips and then frowned at the empty container. "The game's not paused!" he bellowed over his shoulder.

"I know. It's just half-time," she yelled back.

Less than a minute later, the woman marched triumphantly down the hallway with a manila folder in her hands. She snagged the twenty from Jack's hand. "Amanda moved to Kissimmee."

"Florida? Are you sure?" Jack took his notebook back out.

The woman opened up the worn folder in her hands. "That's what the return address says. We had a problem with the furnace after the sale—"

"Problem?" The man swung his arms wide and his belly bounced. "The piece of junk had a crack in the ceramic lining. I had to get a whole new one. Amanda didn't disclose—"

"Just go get another beer." The woman waved her hand as if she were shooing off a fly, and the man shuffled down the hallway.

"Can I get that address?" Jack angled his head to see the envelope. "Amanda Holt?"

"Yeah." The woman's lips pressed together and opened with a pop. "Oh, I remember. Holt. That's her maiden name. She sold the house because she was getting a divorce. Muldoon was her husband's name."

Jack wrote the address down and flicked his notebook closed. A smile spread across his face. "Thank you very much." He turned and headed down the walk.

"Why are you looking for Amanda?" the woman called after him.

"My girlfriend needs something. Amanda's the only one who has it."

3

AVIOPHOBIA

Alice scooted down the crowded airplane. "Do you want the window or the aisle?"

"Aisle." Jack frowned as he looked at the space between rows. "Wait a second." He touched her shoulder. "There are three seats in our row. So why would my choices be window and aisle?"

Alice smiled sheepishly. "At least I got us in the same row."

"Same row, but someone's going to be sitting between us?"

"It's the best I could do. The flight's full." Alice slid over to the window and put her bag beneath the seat in front of her.

"This trip just keeps getting better," Jack grumbled. He jammed his bag into the overhead compartment and wedged his six-foot-one frame into the seat.

"I know!" Alice's pretty face lit up. She was either unaware of his sarcasm or ignoring it. "I can't believe we could change flights on such short notice."

Jack watched her swing her feet. At a fit five-foot-four, Alice had leg room to spare. He tucked his jacket under the seat in front of him—in case Alice got cold later—and then pretended to look at the in-flight magazine. But really, he was watching Alice out of the corner of his eye. She was nervous about meeting his parents and had been a wreck the past two weeks getting ready for the trip. For the hundredth time, Jack wished he'd just rescheduled the trip for later. Alice meeting his parents was awkward enough without trying to explain their situation.

Alice lightly placed her hand over his wrist. Jack glanced down at his hand and realized he was crushing the in-flight magazine.

"Don't tell me you're worried about flying," she said.

"No." Jack stuffed the magazine into the seatback. "I was just thinking about the debacle in the diner."

"Stop calling it that."

"What would *you* call a rejected marriage proposal?"

Alice's green eyes rounded. "I didn't reject it."

"You didn't say yes."

"Jack…"

"I know. It wasn't a 'no'—it was a 'think about it.'"

"But *you* think about it." Alice pointed at him. "You know I love you beyond words. I just don't know if *you* thought the whole thing through. Marriage is huge. It's forever.

I don't want you asking me because you think that's what I want. You should ask me because that's what you want. And because you're ready for it," she quickly added.

"Ready for it? You sound like you're about to throw something at me."

"Some people say marriage is like that. A lot of stuff comes flying your way. That's all I meant when I said not now."

"You said no."

"I said not now." Alice put her feet on the floor. "Look at it from my point of view. There I am eating pancakes, and you're like, marry me? You almost made me choke to death."

"It was spontaneous. I didn't think about it."

"That's the problem. You need to really think it through. That's all I'm saying."

"What—"

A hand touched Jack on the shoulder. "Excuse me."

Jack turned. A very large, round woman with silver hair smiled down at him. She reminded Jack of Mrs. Claus, if Santa's wife helped herself to all the milk and cookies left out for her husband. In her hands was a dog carrier, its top open and the head of a fluffy, cotton-white poodle sticking out.

The woman pointed to the seat between Jack and Alice.

Jack stood and flashed a grin that he hoped was a mix of please-help-me and I'd-sure-appreciate-it. "Good morning, ma'am. Actually, I was hoping we might be able to switch seats. You see—"

The woman's rosy cheeks went pale. Her whole body quivered as she shook her head. "I'm sorry, but I'm just not able. I have aviophobia. Fear of flying."

Alice reached for her seat belt. "Would you like the window?"

The woman's silver bob shook again. "I also have a bit of agoraphobia, but thank you."

"Agoraphobia?" Alice repeated.

"Fear of sweaters?" Jack joked.

The woman cracked a smile. "No. It's an uneasiness with open spaces, so the window wouldn't do."

Alice reached up and started to pull the window shade closed, but the woman's hand shot out like a panicked crossing guard. "Open's fine. Mild claustrophobia."

Jack stepped into the aisle, and the woman wiggled and wedged her way into the middle seat. Alice gave Jack a thin smile. He wanted to finish their conversation about the engagement, but he wasn't about to do it with Mrs. Kringle sitting between them.

"Sorry." The woman let out a little chuckle. "I'm just a big ol' bundle of phobias, but that's why Didi's here."

The little poodle yapped once at the mention of her name.

Alice melted. "She's adorable."

"She's my emotional support animal. She has a vest, but she doesn't like to wear it."

"Maybe she has vestobia," Jack said.

The woman turned to Alice. "Do you like dogs?"

"I love them!" Alice reached out and scratched behind Didi's ears. The little poodle practically purred.

"Wonderful." The woman shifted Didi's carrier and took out a seat belt extender. Even with the extra length, she struggled to click her seat belt around her. After a few failed attempts, she held the dog carrier out toward Jack.

Her smile disappeared when she saw Jack's apprehensive look.

Alice reached out and took the carrier. Didi wiggled at the attention.

"I take it your man's not a dog lover?" the woman whispered loudly to Alice.

"No. He is." Alice's brown ponytail swayed as she nodded. "It just takes Jack a little bit to warm up. I'm Alice."

"Connie Gibson." She smiled triumphantly as the seat belt clicked into place.

Jack tried to twist away from her to give her room, but he was still pressed awkwardly against Connie's shoulder. "I just have a dash of dogophobia."

Apparently oblivious to Jack's joke, Connie settled into her seat.

Fifteen minutes later, the plane was in the air and on its way.

"Are you going to Florida for business or pleasure?" Connie asked Alice.

"Pleasure." Alice turned away from the window. "For a week. We're going to see Jack's parents. They're just getting back from a cruise."

"Oh, that's lovely. I've always wanted to go on a cruise, but…"

"Aquaphobia?" Jack guessed.

"Oh, no. I love the water, but I heard the cabins are just tiny. My friend Lidia said it was like showering in a toilet. And they can be *expensive*."

"My parents won the trip," Jack said. "All expenses paid."

"I'm sure they had a fabulous time." Connie shifted her arms, and Didi leapt out of the carrier and onto Jack's lap. She put her paws against his chest and licked his face.

"Oh, she likes you." Connie didn't move to pick up the dog. "She's giving you kisses."

Jack held the dog away from him with one hand and wiped his cheek with the other. "Here you go."

Connie quickly took the poodle back. "But she's such a little angel!" She held the dog up and Didi licked Connie's puckered mouth.

Jack felt his lip curl and his stomach flip.

"Do you have a dog?" Connie asked Alice.

Alice fidgeted in her seat. "Actually…" Her voice trailed off and she peered over the seat in front of her.

Jack followed her gaze to the front of the plane. The stewardess was hurrying down the aisle. There was still a smile on her face, but it was strained, and Jack could see the concern masked there. She passed them, moving toward the back of the plane, and Jack turned to look. In the rear of the plane, several passengers were waving the stewardess toward them.

Jack undid his seat belt and stood.

From somewhere in the belly of the plane came a low rumble.

Jack froze. The sound grew so loud that everyone in the cabin turned their heads, trying to guess the cause.

Jack sat back in his seat and stared straight ahead. He didn't need to try to figure out what was making the noise. He knew exactly what it was—and it was very, very bad.

"What on earth could that be?" Connie clutched Didi tightly to her bosom.

Jack leaned forward to look at Alice. A mixture of heartbreak and concern was etched across her face. He knew she wanted to run to the cargo hold.

Suddenly, loud barks boomed and echoed from deep within the plane, followed by a long howl that made everyone on the plane sit up nervously.

Murmured questions raced through the plane.

"What are they transporting?"

"Is it safe?"

"It's too loud to be a dog. Wolves?"

Jack sat back in his seat and took out the in-flight magazine.

"What do you think it is?" Connie asked, wide-eyed. "Aren't you worried?"

Jack grinned. "You've got nothing to worry about. I do. But you? You're fine."

Connie turned her puzzled look to Alice.

"What Jack means is…" Alice wrung her hands. "That's our dog. Lady."

"The creature making that tremendous noise is a *dog*?"

Alice nodded. "She's a King Shepherd. See, I had a doggy boarding home all picked out, but when we went to drop Lady off…the place was horrible. It was dirty, and someone was yelling at the dogs, and I just couldn't leave Lady there. I just couldn't."

Connie patted Alice's hand. "Neither would I. Not on your life. You are a good momma to your fur baby. I understand completely."

"And there was just no one else to watch her. Mrs. Stevens, our landlady, is away taking care of her sister, so we *had* to bring her."

"Is she in cargo?"

Alice's lip quivered. "They said she'd be okay there. I asked the vet, and he promised she'd be fine."

Connie squeezed her hand. "Is this her first time flying?"

Alice nodded.

"She's okay," Jack said. "She'll settle down in a couple of minutes."

"Are you sure?" Alice asked hopefully.

"Positive." Jack clicked his tongue. "Give her a couple of minutes and she'll start thinking of all the ways she's going to get even with me for taking her on this trip. She'll forget all about the plane and spend the rest of the flight plotting her revenge."

4

RULE NUMBER ONE

Dixon strolled across the living room of his aunt's house, carrying a box of chocolate-covered macadamia nuts. "Did you miss me, Auntie?"

His aunt sat in a wingback chair with a martini glass delicately balanced in two fingers. Her blue eyes studied him as he plopped the candies onto the coffee table. "Your shoes are filthy. Either clean them properly or remove them before you enter my house."

Dixon glanced around the room, filled with items imported from around the globe; most had come via Beverly Hills boutiques. He shook his head and whistled low. "Look at all this pricey stuff." He slid into the seat opposite her, put his feet up on the table next to the candies, and folded his hands behind his head. "You might be wiping your butt with silk now, but you had the same trailer crib as my mom and me, you know." Dixon inhaled deeply. "So don't go—"

He stopped abruptly when he saw the silver Glock in her hands.

"Get your feet off my table, stand up, and address me properly like a big boy and not some redneck trash."

Dixon laughed. It came straight from the gut and made his shoulders bounce. "You're one hot ticket, Auntie. Mom always said if she was a firecracker, you were dynamite."

"You think I won't shoot you because you're my sister's son? The *only* reason I'm not shooting you is that I like this carpet. It's an antique Persian Sarouk. Now get your damn feet off my Leroux table."

Dixon stood, flicked from the table a clump of mud that had fallen from his sneaker, and smiled. "Happy?"

His aunt set the gun down in her lap and sipped her martini.

"You know you can text me the address, right?" he said.

Seeing the expression on his aunt's face, Dixon was glad she had put the gun down before he said that.

"Don't write anything down—*ever*. A couple is coming in tonight: 11 Banyan Breeze Drive."

Dixon waited. He knew he was in for a scolding after the old soldier went and had a heart attack. It was why he'd brought the chocolates. But as he stood there, anticipating a lecture, his aunt simply stared at him and sipped her martini.

Dixon ran his hands through his hair. "Aren't you going to give me crap about the last guy?"

She glanced down at the gun, smiled, and sipped her martini. "I've made what is required of you perfectly clear: don't bring unwanted attention. You're my sister's child, but if I continue to think that you could alter my situation here, you'll find out that all those stories my sister told you about me were true."

Dixon felt the vein in his temple begin to throb. He liked his aunt, but he had rules. And rule number one was: no one threatens him. *No one.* Still, right now, she was making the money rain, and he wasn't about to shut off that faucet. "Anything you say, Auntie." He sarcastically blew her a kiss and headed to the door.

"I also want you to stay clean."

"I'm not using," Dixon lied. He couldn't wait to get to his car and take a hit to kill the pounding in his head. "Does this couple have a name?" he called over his shoulder.

"Stratton. Ted and Laura Stratton."

5

NOT MY IDEA

The bright-green compact rental car, with two suitcases strapped to its roof, sped straight down the palm tree-lined street. Lady took up the entire backseat of the tiny car, resting her head on her paws.

Alice looked at the map on her phone and pointed left. "There it is."

Jack turned at the wide wooden sign: *Orange Blossom Cove.*

"It's a fifty-five-plus community with senior care," Jack explained. "My mom's cousin lived here until she died and left it to my mom. With my father's declining health, it was a huge blessing. They'd never have been able to afford it otherwise."

"It's a gated community. That sounds safe."

Jack pulled up to the white bar that crossed the road and served as a gate. "It *sounds* safe, but it isn't really." He pointed at the bar. "You kind of need a *wall* to go with the *gate* to make it safe. Without a wall, you can just go around the gate." He powered down his window, and the hot, humid air rushed in as if he'd opened an oven door. "It's Martian-hot here."

Jack took a deep breath of the tropical air and looked at the landscaped entrance with palms and some kind of mini trees covered in pink flowers. "They spend more money on flowers than security. They need a wall and a guard. I'd add a patrol, too."

"So you want your parents to move to an army base?"

"An army base would be safer." Jack punched in the code his father had given him and the white bar slowly rose. Jack powered his window back up and reached for the air-conditioning knob, but it was already running at full blast. "It's like living in a humidifier," he grumbled. "How can my dad stand it?"

They took a left at a single-story building with a large circular dome in its center. A half dozen cars were parked out front. Jack pointed at it. "The community center makes this a great setup for my parents. They really don't have to go anywhere now. They have doctors who have office hours in there, and a gym. Their groceries are delivered, and someone checks in on them."

As they crossed a stone bridge, they had a great view of the community. Three small ponds were connected by a canal, and over a dozen white homes with terracotta-tiled roofs surrounded each pond. Some were single units, but most were duplexes.

They took two more turns before arriving at the Strattons' single-family house. It was identical to the other cookie-cutter Florida homes except for the bouquet of balloons and a sign hung over the front door: *Welcome Home!*

Alice beamed. "Your mom is awesome."

"She is." Jack parked in the driveway.

"Do I look all right?" Alice smoothed out her new summer dress, white with blue roses. She had spent hours picking it out and finding a pair of shoes that were just right.

"You're beautiful. And stop worrying—my parents don't care what you look like."

Alice nodded, but she still reached for the visor and checked her reflection in the mirror.

He climbed out of the car and opened the back door just as Alice blurted out, "No, wait!"

Lady bounded from the car and landed with her feet wide and her paws digging into the grass. A low growl rumbled deep in her chest as she turned her head to glare at Jack.

Jack raised a hand. "It wasn't my idea to put you on the plane."

Lady started marching toward him.

Jack started backpedaling.

Alice raced around the car. "Lady! Lady, it's okay."

"It wasn't my idea!" Jack held both hands up and kept shuffling backward.

Lady barked twice and shook her head; the ripple traveled along her back, raising her fur. Puffed up like that, she looked even larger than her one hundred and twenty pounds.

"She doesn't know that, Jack." Alice grabbed the thick collar and planted her feet, but Lady easily dragged her forward.

"Seriously, dog, you're blaming the wrong person here."

"She can't understand you, Jack."

"She understands me just fine. Look! She shook her head!" Jack was backed up almost to the front door. "She just doesn't believe me."

Once Jack was trapped between her and the house, Lady stopped walking and instead began to bark.

"See?" Jack yelled over the noise. "She's chewing me out!"

After another minute, Lady's mouth snapped shut. With a snort, as if signaling that she had finished, she started to walk away, dragging Alice after her.

Alice managed to clip the leash onto the collar. "I'll just let her stretch her legs," she called back before she disappeared around the corner.

Jack exhaled. "Great. We were buddies before this trip, and now she wants to eat me." He knocked on the front door of his parents' house.

He waited.

Just before he knocked again, an older woman hurried across the yard from the house next door. She looked to be in her mid-sixties, and her hair was an odd shade of reddish-brown that clashed with her polka-dotted pink summer dress. She walked with her right hand raised in front of her and her mouth open, ready to speak from the moment she left her house.

"Are you looking for the Strattons?"

She stopped with her waist and knees slightly bent and her head thrust forward on her long neck. Jack thought she looked like one of those shore birds that move through the ponds with one eye on the fish and one eye on people, ready to spear one or the other with their pointy beak.

"Yes, I'm their—"

"They're not home. What was that *thing* that came out of your car? They don't allow exotic animals here, and I'm sure—"

Jack interrupted. This woman's brusque manner and nasal voice chafed him. "She's not a thing. She's a dog."

The woman's mouth closed with a pop. Her hands went to her hips and she spoke down her nose at Jack. "That's not a dog."

"She's a King Shepherd—a big softie. Excuse me." Jack took out his phone and dialed his father.

"Regardless, we have a leash law."

"She's on a leash."

"She was not on a leash. You should have control of your animal at all times, and that beast is bigger than your wife."

Jack could hear a phone ringing inside his parents' house. His father's voicemail picked up again. "Wonderful," he muttered.

The woman must have heard the phone ringing too. She folded her arms across her chest and smiled smugly.

"Do you happen to know where they might be?" Jack asked.

"They're probably at the community center. A lot of people here waste time playing bingo. I guess it's okay if you have nothing better to do."

Jack bristled. He was about to give her a piece of his mind but stopped short. Perhaps it was because of his proximity to his parents' house, but he could almost feel his mother's reproving stare. He forced himself to act cordially to their neighbor. "Thank you." He held out his hand. "I'm Jack Stratton."

"Oh." The woman shook his hand and eyed him like an appraiser on *Antiques Road Trip*. "So, you're the one Laura is always going on about."

"That's my mom."

"I'm Gladys Crouse. Are you staying with them?"

"Actually, I think I'm going to head over to that community center. Nice meeting you."

"If you stay overnight, you need to check in and get a visitor's pass." Her eyes suddenly widened. "And guests aren't allowed to have animals."

Without responding, Jack walked in the direction Alice and Lady had gone. As he rounded the corner of the house, he spotted them taking long strides along a brick path that encircled the pond behind his parents' home.

Jack cupped his hands to his mouth and called, "I'm heading over to the community center! My parents are there!"

Alice waved and nodded.

As Jack headed down the block toward the community center, Gladys stood in her doorway and watched him go.

Guests aren't allowed to have animals? Did she memorize the community handbook?

His parents' car was parked in front of the community center. Jack had no trouble spotting it; the "I Love My Math Teacher" bumper sticker was a dead giveaway.

As he walked through the wide glass doors, a woman in a sharp business suit strode forward. Her dark-gray jacket and white blouse had more of a Wall Street look than Orange Blossom Cove.

"May I help you?" Her heels clicked on the tiled section of floor in front of the door. She stopped in front of Jack and blocked his forward progress.

"I'm Jack Stratton. I was told that my parents are at bingo. Ted and Laura Stratton."

"Certainly. Please follow me." She turned and walked to another set of glass double doors.

Jack followed her into a large multipurpose room filled with elderly people sitting at rows of tables.

"N thirty-seven!" The announcer held up a Ping-Pong ball he'd just plucked from what looked like a giant hamster ball. The number was projected in enormous digits on two screens for all to see. The whole setup was in front of a small theatrical stage with sparkling silver curtains on both sides.

The announcer made a big show of turning a crank handle that started the giant hamster ball turning. The numbered balls inside it bounced back and forth. After a moment, he stopped cranking, pulled out another selection, and held it high. "I twenty-one!"

Murmurs, mutterings, and a couple of hopeful pleadings flittered around the room.

An older woman strolled over to Jack and Miss Wall Street. "Is everything all right, Tia?"

"Yes, Mrs. Miller," Tia replied. "Mr. Stratton is looking for his parents."

The woman's smile was warm and her gray eyes were bright. "You must be Jack." She shook his hand. "Your folks are right over here. Thank you, Tia."

Tia tilted her head and walked back out the door.

"I'm Helen Miller." The woman took Jack by the arm as if he were an old friend. "I don't think your poor father has even had a chance to unpack from their cruise, but your mother insisted on coming down and thanking everyone for their trip. She's the most thoughtful woman."

Jack chuckled. His mother was always the first to fire off a thank-you card for even the slightest gesture. "My mom said they had a great time and she's very grateful."

"Well, we're grateful for them. Your parents are a delightful addition to our community."

Helen patted Jack's arm, and her diamond rings glittered. Jack glanced at her white pantsuit; he could have sworn it was the same Armani outfit that Alice had pointed out in the in-flight magazine. He tried to push the thought aside, but he couldn't help but wonder how much money all the people staying here must be spending if the head of the community center could afford to dress like a cross between a CEO and a fashion designer.

The ball in the front of the room stopped spinning. "N forty-two!"

"*Bingo!* Me! Bingo! Yay!" A woman's hands shot into the air.

A few players politely clapped. Jack stifled a grin at all the grumpy faces.

"They're a competitive lot," he whispered.

"You don't know the half of it," Helen whispered back. "Because of regulations, we don't play for cash. But all bingo club members get a chance to win the drawing at the end of the month. It gives them something to look forward to."

"You sure give out a big prize. I couldn't believe my parents won a cruise."

"That's not the monthly prize, that's the *grand* prize. You need to get a triple-decker to win the cruise."

"A what?"

"A triple-decker. That's three full houses in a row."

Apparently, bingo was just finishing up, as the crowd stood and began to disperse. Jack spotted his parents in the corner. "There they are," Jack said.

His mother hadn't seen him yet and moved toward the bingo table at the front of the room. But his father saw him and waved him and Helen over.

Jack's father, Ted Stratton, still dressed as if he were about to teach a math class—khaki pants and a crisp, white button-down shirt.

"Hi, Dad. Sorry we're late."

His dad gave him a bear hug. "Alice isn't with you?"

"She's back at your house. I just left you a message."

Ted smiled at Helen. "I see you met my son, Jack."

"I was just telling him how lucky your wife is."

"A triple-decker." Ted shook his head. "Mathematically, it's like getting hit by lightning."

"Explain that to my manager." Helen rolled her eyes. "We've given away three cruises in two months. I find myself holding my breath at every game."

"Jack!" his mother called out. He looked over to see her dragging the announcer by the hand through the crowd.

She gave Jack a hug. "When did you get in? Where's Alice?"

"She's back at the house. I—"

"We should get going right away then. I'm so sorry I wasn't there. I just had to stop in and thank Mr. Pitman." She turned to the announcer, a tall man in a beige suit. "This is Mr. Pitman. He gave us the trip."

The announcer blushed to the top of his bald head. "You won it, Laura. I'm just glad you had a nice time." He held out a hand to Jack. "Marvin. Pleasure."

"Jack." As Jack shook the man's hand, he realized the end of Marvin's index finger was missing.

Marvin made a comical face. "Sorry for the handshake. Bingo ball bit the knuckle off." He rolled his eyes. "Oh, wait, it was Mrs. Landing who bit it off when she lost."

Ted chuckled and gave Jack a wink.

"Well, thank you again." Laura grinned. "It really was wonderful."

"Don't thank me." Marvin gestured toward Helen. "Helen lets me have the games here. And as long as we do, we'll keep having winners."

"I'd never dream of stopping bingo, Marvin. I think there'd be a riot!" Helen laughed.

"Thank you too, Helen." Laura moved behind Jack and his father and prodded them to the door. "We shouldn't keep Alice waiting."

The men gladly weaved quickly through the crowd and back into the summer heat.

Ted handed Jack a handkerchief. "I've adjusted to the heat, so how about you use this one."

Jack was embarrassed to use a handkerchief—it seemed like an old man thing—but he took it and wiped his brow. "Thanks. You look great, Dad. You've lost a lot of weight."

"Thirty pounds. But it's all water weight. Sweat. Living in a steam room has that effect on you." His father wiped his hand from his forehead over the top of his bald head for emphasis.

"Oh, Ted." Laura gave Jack a faux look of exasperation. "He's doing great with his training. Your father goes for a walk every morning and watches every bite. I'm very proud of him."

"Do you like how she tries to spin it by calling it 'training'?" Ted opened the passenger-side door for his wife. "She calls it training like I'm preparing for the Olympics. It's more like obedience training. She gives me little treats and I do her bidding."

Laura leaned in close to her husband and whispered, "I thought you *liked* my reward system."

"I'm right here, Mom." Jack felt his cheeks redden. "A little too much information."

Ted chuckled and nudged Jack. "You're old enough now, Jack."

"No, Dad, I'm not. There are some things you're never old enough for. The method Mom is using to motivate you to lose weight is one of those things."

They settled into their seats. Ted drove, with Laura in the passenger seat and Jack in the back.

Laura immediately turned around and started firing off questions faster than Marvin called bingo numbers. "Did you just get in? How was your flight? Is the rental car big enough? Did you get any sleep on the plane?"

Jack covered everything about the trip except one little detail—Lady. Before he could figure out a way to explain that he had to bring a giant dog with him, they pulled into the driveway.

Jack cleared his throat. "Ah…did you guys happen to listen to your messages when you got home?"

His father took a deep breath. "No, but by the sound of your tone I have a feeling that I should have."

Jack chuckled nervously. "Kinda. I called, but you were in the Bahamas, and… Well, we had a slight issue back in Darrington before we left."

As Jack's dad got out of the car, his mom whispered, "Is everything okay?"

"That depends."

"Jack, what's wrong?"

Ted crossed over to open the door for Laura. He glanced around. "Where's Alice?"

Jack got out. "She's here. But we also had to bring—"

Lady suddenly bounded around the corner of the house and headed straight for Jack, barking nonstop.

Ted stepped between the charging dog and his son. He pulled himself up to his full five-foot-five height and commanded, *"Sit!"*

Lady skidded to a stop and sat down.

Jack stood there, blinking, as if he'd just seen a magician make a woman vanish before his eyes. "How'd you do that?"

"Jack…" Ted didn't take his eyes off the enormous dog in front of him. "Slowly back up and get in the car."

"Dad, it's—"

"Shh… Don't talk. Slowly get in the car." Ted started to back up. "Don't make any sudden moves."

"It's okay, Dad," Jack said. "It's my dog."

"Is that Lady?" Jack expected his mother to faint, but she hurried out of the car. "She's adorable."

Lady seemed to forget all about Jack. Her back arched high as Laura scratched behind her ears. She pressed against Jack's mother and wagged her tail.

"Lady!" Alice called from somewhere behind the house.

Ted's glasses lifted from his nose as one eyebrow arched high. "That's not a dog. It's something out of *The Lord of the Rings*."

"Lady!" Alice flew around the corner of the house and slowed to a stop. Her knees were dirty, her new dress was torn at the hem, and several leaves dangled from her brown ponytail. Her face flushed bright crimson. "Hi, Mr. and Mrs. Stratton." She offered an embarrassed one-handed wave as she walked forward and grabbed Lady's collar.

"Alice." Laura looked her up and down with a sympathetic frown and gave her a big hug. "Are you okay, honey?"

Alice nodded as she tucked an errant strand of hair back in place. "We were around the far side of the pond. Lady saw Jack in the car and took off. I managed to hang on when she jumped a little fence, but when she charged through a wall of bushes, I got stuck." She held up a length of frayed, broken nylon cording in her free hand. "Stupid leash."

"Alice." Ted smiled, and Jack could tell he was trying to stifle a chuckle. "It's nice to see you in person. I'd shake your hand, but I'm worried about losing it if I get too close to your werewolf."

Alice sighed. "She's harmless...unless you try to hold on when she decides to run."

The window on the house next door slid up, and Gladys stuck her head out. "Laura! Laura Stratton!" She wiggled one finger like a reed in a hurricane. "Guests are not allowed to bring wild animals."

Ted waved. "That's not quite right, Mrs. Crouse. But thanks for telling us."

"Even if they *could* bring a dog," Gladys continued, "I'm sure they're supposed to be properly restrained."

Alice paled and tightened her grip on Lady's collar. "I'm sorry, ma'am. She broke her leash and—"

"That's no surprise considering the size of that beast. It looks dangerous."

"She's a wonderful dog," Laura protested.

"And they don't have a parking tag." Gladys pointed at the rental car. "They have to check in at the office if they're staying overnight. When they do, make sure they ask if that...that *thing* is allowed."

"All righty, Mrs. Crouse." Ted bowed, making a show of it. When he straightened, he smiled and gave her a sweeping wave. "You have a nice day."

"They're not staying overnight?" Gladys asked.

"Nice seeing you, Mrs. Crouse." Ted whispered to Jack, lips as motionless as a ventriloquist's, "When she sticks her head in, pull your car into the garage."

"I'm going to call the main office to check about the dog," Gladys threatened. She shut the window hard and disappeared.

Ted hurried to the garage door. "Pull it in now!"

Jack hesitated.

"Don't just stand there, Jack. She's calling the clubhouse and the phone's on the other side of her house. She won't see you pull in."

Jack jumped into the rental car and parked in the garage next to his mother's car. "Why don't we just check in?" he asked as he exited the garage.

"Just in case they do have some silly rule about dogs and overnight guests. Sometimes it's better to ask for forgiveness than permission."

Jack's jaw dropped in sync with the garage door behind him. "Dad, I could have used that tip when I was seventeen."

Ted laughed and gave him a playful shot in the arm. "Some advice has to wait until the recipient has the maturity to understand it."

Jack pointed at Gladys's house. "Do you really think she'll complain?"

"I guarantee it. She lives for making other people's lives miserable."

"You sure were polite to her."

"Killing her with kindness. So far, it's not working. She's still not nice, and she's still breathing."

Laura draped a comforting arm around Alice's shoulders. "Why don't we all go in and get settled?"

"You're sure it's okay for Lady to stay here?" Jack asked.

Alice's neck lengthened and she shot Jack a disbelieving glance.

"Of course!" Laura patted Lady's head. "She's just as welcome as you are."

The inside of the Strattons' home was typical Floridian: high ceilings, tile, fans, and central air running full blast. The single-floor home had a living room to the right, a bright kitchen in the back, and two rooms off a little hallway on the left.

Lady's claws clicked off the tile as she sniffed excitedly and pushed open each door to look around.

"I have the guest bedroom all set up for you, Alice." Laura pointed left. "And we'll make up the couch for you, Jack."

"I'll be fine out here. Jack can have the bedroom," Alice offered.

Jack shook his head. "Sorry, babe, not an option. Don't even try. My mom wouldn't hear of it."

Laura patted his cheek. "I wouldn't. I have sweet tea in the kitchen. I think I'm getting the hang of making it. Ted, why don't you give me a hand while they get settled?"

"You'd like me to give you a hand making tea that's already made?"

Laura pulled him toward the kitchen. "They just got off the plane, and they don't need us crowding them," she whispered.

Ted turned to Alice. "I cleared out a bureau. Make yourselves at home. Does the grizzly bear need anything?"

Alice shook her head. "We stopped and picked up food. Are you sure it's okay if Lady stays, Mr. Stratton? We could try—"

"Of course she can stay. And call me Ted."

Laura tugged on his arm again and succeeded in drawing Jack's father down the hallway.

"Make yourselves at home!" Ted called back.

As soon as he was out of sight, Alice spun around. Her words were low and clipped. Each one popped. "You didn't ask if Lady could stay *before* we got here?"

"I—"

"You told me that you called them."

From the red tinge at the top of her ears, Jack could tell that she was more embarrassed by the breach of etiquette than she was angry. "I did call, but my dad must have his phone in airplane mode or on silent. I left a couple of messages."

"Asking if a one hundred twenty-pound dog can stay at their house warrants more than a message." She put her hands on her hips. "You need to speak to them."

Jack tilted his head and studied her pose. "You look just like Aunt Haddie when you stand like that."

"Seriously? I wanted to make a good first impression, and *that* wasn't it." Alice sniffed and looked away.

"You don't have to impress my parents. They already love you." Jack draped an arm around her shoulders and gave her a squeeze.

"They don't know me."

"True…" Jack joked.

Alice elbowed his ribs and held back a grin. "Be nice or I'll tell Lady that the plane really was all your idea."

At the mention of her name, Lady turned around. Her big brown eyes connected with Jack's. She stared at him for a moment before she let out a satisfied huff.

"There." Alice leaned her head against Jack's chest. "I think she's forgiven you."

"Ha." Jack frowned. "She wasn't saying that. She was saying something like, 'You'd better sleep with one eye open because I'm going to pay you back for the plane.'"

Alice laughed. "Don't be silly."

Lady trotted to the bedroom door. She turned around, stared at Jack, and huffed again. But this time, Jack swore she smiled.

6

BEWARE OF ALLIGATORS

Ted pointed at the sign posted a few yards away, close to Gladys's property line. It read: *Beware of Alligators*.

"Don't worry though. If you leave them alone, they leave you alone."

Jack stopped to study the water. "Have you seen any?"

"From a distance. I saw one walk across the Johnsons' yard one time." Ted pointed four doors down and then walked back toward the house. "It looked like a dinosaur."

Jack stared a moment, nodding, and then caught up with his dad outside the lanai. "You need a gun."

"What? I'm not hunting them."

"Not just for the alligators." Jack pointed at the sign. "That sign is going to keep you and Mom safe about as well as the so-called 'gate' at the front of this place."

"I don't need a gun."

"Statistically, you being older and—"

"I have two."

"Seriously, Dad. I know the crime rate is low, but I think—"

"I *am* serious. I got one for myself and one for your mother."

"You bought Mom a gun?" Jack felt his eyebrows traveling in different directions. "I can picture her holding a plate of cookies, but not a gun."

Ted looked around as though they were about to be caught doing something bad. "Good thing Alice isn't around to hear that. Your mother's a better shot with a gun than I am. And of *course* I got her one too. Let me give you a life lesson, son. Your mother and I, we have each other's back. That's what marriage is all about, right?"

At the mention of marriage, Jack cleared his throat and changed the subject. "This whole retirement community setup is awesome. Anything else you want to show me?"

"Nope. That's the end of the tour." Ted opened the back door, and the two of them went inside.

Alice and Laura sat at the kitchen table, flipping through the pages of a photo album. A stack of five more sat at Laura's elbow.

Alice looked up and clapped her hands in delight. "You were so cute."

Jack groaned. "Mom, don't embarrass me."

"I would never dream of it, dear." She turned back to the photos. "Jack was eight," she explained. "School was doing a Thanksgiving Day play."

"Not *that* picture..." Jack leaned against the counter.

Ted handed him an iced tea. "Artificial sweetener," he whispered and stuck out his tongue.

"It's nothing to be embarrassed about," Laura continued. "Mrs. Swanson did a fabulous job on your costume."

"I was a turkey."

Alice's feet tapped the floor like a rock drummer doing a solo. "You were an adorable turkey."

"And this is Jack and Ted performing." Laura pointed at a picture of the two of them on a stage.

"Were they in a play?" Alice asked.

"It's actually a comedy routine." Ted tipped an imaginary hat. "Like Abbott and Costello."

"Abbott and Costello were two vaudeville comedians," Laura explained. "These days they're mostly known for a silly skit called 'Who's on First?' but they did a number of movies."

"Long before your time," Ted said.

"Anyway, Ted and Jack won first place!" Laura said proudly.

Jack sighed and shook his head. "It was a junior high talent show, Mom, not *America's Got Talent*."

"It was still first place. They did a math skit," she said to Alice. "It was hilarious. Only Ted could make math funny. He's been teaching again, you know."

"I thought the doctors wanted you to take it easy, Dad."

Ted took off his glasses and started to clean them. He glanced up at Jack and then back down. "Well, down here there isn't that much to do, so I've been doing a little tutoring. Volunteer. It's just a few hours a week."

Jack's mother shook her head. "It's more than a few hours. He even started raising money for a scholarship for inner-city children." His mother raised her eyebrows. "The Chandler Carter Math Scholarship."

Jack coughed and pinched the bridge of his nose. His foster brother Chandler had wanted to be a math teacher, but died serving in Iraq. An image flashed in Jack's mind, of Chandler smiling like a kid at Christmas. That his dad would start a scholarship in Chandler's name made Jack proud, but any thought of Chandler also made his chest hurt.

Alice squeezed Jack's hand. "That's very nice of you, Mr. Stratton."

Ted turned to his wife. "Time to change the subject, Laura. You're embarrassing both me *and* Jack. So, how was the plane ride, Jack?"

Jack scanned the kitchen and then cocked his head, listening. "Wait. Where's Lady?"

"In the guest room." Alice pouted. "She doesn't want to come out."

"Why not?"

"She's scared."

Ted chuckled. "What could scare that dog?" He opened a cabinet.

Laura shook her head. "Ted, you just had a snack," she held up her phone, "twenty minutes ago."

"I was just getting…some ice water." Ted took down a glass. He leaned over and whispered in Jack's ear. "The CIA has nothing on your mother. I nibble on a cracker and she knows it."

Laura crossed her arms. "You asked me to keep you on track."

"I think I was too weak from hunger when I made that request."

"Don't be silly. I sliced vegetables and put them on the bottom shelf if you can't wait."

"Do you know Laura's secret to getting me to lose weight?" Ted asked Alice.

Alice shook her head.

"She ties pork chops to my ankles and makes me walk around the pond. I have to run for fear the alligators will get me! But if I make it home alive, she cooks up the pork chops for lunch. Those pounds fall right off!"

Alice glanced up uncertainly at Jack, who cracked up laughing, along with his father.

Jack rubbed Alice's blushing neck. "Really though. What's Lady scared of?"

"Geckos. She went out to the lanai, saw one, and freaked out."

"Beast is afraid of a little lizard?" Jack laughed again.

"Totally freaked out. She ran into the living room, and just her luck, there's a statue of a gecko on the mantel. She started barking her head off at it."

"The poor baby," Laura said.

"Baby is right," Jack said. "Scared of a tiny gecko."

The sounds of claws tapping against the tile floor announced Lady's entrance into the kitchen. She was chewing on something wide enough to stick out both sides of her mouth. It flopped up each time she brought her powerful jaws down.

"Oh, Lady…" Alice said, her voice rising.

Lady opened her mouth, and the remains of a drool-covered sneaker plopped onto the tile with a wet smack.

"My new running shoes!" Jack's hands went to the sides of his head.

Lady let out a satisfied snort and trotted away.

"They cost me over a hundred bucks!" Jack called after her. "I'm taking it out of your food!"

"Maybe I can clean it," Alice said.

"No. Beast mangled it."

Alice picked up the sopping-wet shoe. "I can wash it."

Ted put a comforting hand on her shoulder. "I'm afraid that shoe is beyond saving."

Alice turned to Laura, who wrinkled her nose and shook her head.

"Toss it." Jack pointed to the trash can. "She nearly tore the heel right off."

"Does Lady have a habit of chewing on things?" Ted asked nervously. He walked down the hall to peer in the guest bedroom.

"You've got nothing to worry about," Jack said. "She only chews on *my* things."

"I think Lady's still upset about the plane ride," Alice explained.

"And now she's turned back into the werewolf that hates me."

"Don't be silly, honey," Laura said. "Dogs chew on things. I'm sure Lady doesn't have a bad bone in her body."

"You have no idea how it was when we first got her. And now I'm back to square one."

"I'll pick you up another pair of sneakers," Alice offered, "and a chew toy for Lady."

"You can hold off on the chew toy." Ted walked back into the kitchen. "Right now, Lady's working out her aggression on Jack's other running shoe."

"Dad! Did you take it away from her?"

"Why? Listen, for one thing, I'm not about to try to get it away from her. I like my hands. Besides, what are you going to do with one sneaker? Maybe she'll think the score is settled after she finishes it off."

Jack was about to protest when the doorbell rang.

Lady started to bark, and Alice shot down the hallway, followed by Jack's mother.

While Alice put Lady back into the bedroom, Laura led a man and three older women into the kitchen. All of them looked to be in their seventies. They smiled, nodded, and waved as Laura lined them up in front of the sink.

Alice slipped back into the kitchen and stood next to Jack.

"This is my son, Jack, and this is his sweet Alice." Laura held her hand out to a short man with gray hair on the sides of his head, covered by an obvious dark-brown toupee. "Jack and Alice, this is Carl Wilkerson."

Carl nodded curtly.

She gestured to the woman next to Carl, who was a couple of inches taller than him. She wore a yellow-and-white-flowered dress with a matching yellow hat, and had long, straight hair. "And this is Ellie Harper."

Ellie wiggled her fingers in a shy greeting.

Laura continued down the line. "Ruby Green." Ruby was a big woman with a thousand-watt smile. When she waved, her bright-plum dress with pale-cobalt flowers shimmered. Her black hair was styled in an elegant bouffant.

"And Ginny Peek."

Ginny looked as if she had just gotten off work from a library in the 1950s: she wore a gray jacket, matching skirt, and white blouse. Glasses dangled from a cord around her neck. Her hair was pulled back in a tight librarian bun, and when she nodded once in greeting, it barely moved.

Ruby was the first to speak. "Let me just say that we're all so glad you'll help."

All four nodded and looked at Jack expectantly.

Jack tensed. "Excuse me?"

Laura tittered. "Oh, he just got in and I haven't had a chance to explain the particulars to him."

What had his mom gotten him into? *Particulars?* Jack wanted to say. *You haven't explained* any*thing.* But he bit his tongue. He would never embarrass his mother in front of her friends.

"Oh, boy, here it comes," Ted muttered. He leaned against the counter next to Jack and sipped his iced tea nonchalantly.

Jack felt the first beads of sweat forming on his forehead.

Laura wrung her hands. "Well...at our last meeting—"

"It wasn't the last one," Ginny corrected her. "It was on the eleventh."

Laura grinned sheepishly. "Thank you, Ginny. Yes, on the eleventh we got together for a brainstorming session."

"At the club," Ellie added.

"The club?" Jack repeated.

"Our book club," Ruby explained.

"The murder and *mystery* book club." Ginny adjusted the cord holding her glasses until they were even on both sides.

Ellie stepped forward. "And we need your help."

Jack sat down on one of the kitchen chairs.

"I told you he's too busy." Carl crossed his arms. "We're close to solving it ourselves anyway."

"Solving what?" Alice asked. "A book mystery?"

"No." Ruby shook her head and leaned against the table as if delivering a secret. "We've got a real-life whodunit."

"A murder?" Alice's eyes widened.

"No." Ellie leaned in like Ruby. "A string of robberies," she whispered.

"They're thefts," Carl corrected her.

"Actually…" Ginny stood up straight, as if she were giving a presentation to a class, "they're burglaries. A burglary is breaking into a building with the intent to steal something inside. A theft is simply taking something that belongs to someone else. And robbery involves violence or threat of violence."

Everyone looked at Jack.

He nodded. "She's correct."

Ginny proudly squared her shoulders.

"But you don't need to break in to commit burglary," Jack added. "Going in through an unlocked window is still burglary. Is someone breaking into homes here?"

"Someone or some*ones*." Ellie raised her eyebrows.

"Someones?" Jack repeated.

"That's her theory." Ruby crossed one arm around her waist while her other hand stroked her chin like a TV detective. "She thinks it's the work of a gang of retired criminals, but *I* think the Orange Blossom Cove Bandit is a woman. She's too cunning and skilled to be a man."

Laura, Carl, Ellie, Ruby, and Ginny suddenly all began talking at once, each defending their own theory or trying to poke holes in someone else's.

"Hold on," Jack said. "Did you go to the police?"

"Several times," Ellie said.

Ruby stood with her hands on her hips. "But they're stumped."

"So there's already a current investigation?"

"Yes, but they're not getting anywhere," Ruby said. "And Laura offered—"

Ted held up his hands. "Which she shouldn't have. Jack's on vacation and here only for a few days."

"Told you he wouldn't help," Carl muttered.

"Look, I'm sure the police here can handle a couple of B&Es." As Jack spoke, he saw his mom's lips press tighter together like they did when she wasn't getting her way. But as her eyes softened in disappointment, so did Jack's resolve. He caved. "If my mom said I'd help—"

"Nope." Ted popped the *p* for emphasis. "You're on vacation and you deserve it. You're not getting involved."

"But what about the burglar?" Ellie moved closer to Carl.

Carl put a protective hand on her shoulder. "There's probably nothing to worry about."

7

I LOVE YOU, LADY

Jack rolled over on the pullout couch. The thin mattress did little to cushion his back from the metal bars that served as a bed frame. The heat only added to his discomfort. He felt as if he were sleeping inside a waffle iron.

"Central air? Where?" Jack grumbled as he folded his hands behind his head. As soon as everyone had shut their bedroom doors, the temperature in the living room had steadily risen until he was sweating just lying there.

He tried relaxing into the unforgiving mattress. Keeping his eyes closed, he focused on the beating of his heart. Finally, he began to slip into sleep.

Lady scratched at the door of the guest bedroom.

Jack hurried out of bed, worried the noise would wake his parents. He cracked open the bedroom door and Lady shoved her way past him.

Alice groggily called out from somewhere in the darkness. "I can take her."

"I've got it. Stay in bed."

Lady sat down on the floor, tilted her head, and gazed up at him. He could have sworn she was smirking.

"You went out an hour ago. You're just doing this to get back at me, right?"

Lady set her huge paw down on Jack's bare foot, her rough pads scraping his bare skin.

"Ow! Okay. For the hundredth time, I'm sorry. But listen, I got you a peace offering. I was going to show you in the morning, but I'll give it to you now if you knock it off and go to bed." Jack headed for the kitchen. "Come on."

It was actually his mother who had picked up a "treat" for Lady, but he wasn't about to tell Lady that. Besides, Jack was the one about to cook it.

As soon as he took the steak tips out of the refrigerator, Lady began to prance in a circle. She knocked the kitchen chairs against the table and tipped the water dish to one side. It righted itself with a metallic clang.

"*Shh*. Wake up my parents and the deal is off."

Lady sat down.

"After this, we're even." Jack put the steak in a large pan. "Besides, it wasn't my idea to bring you on the plane anyway."

At the word "plane," a low grumble began deep in her chest.

"You are a freak of nature, dog. I know you understand me. So, get this: *Alice* brought Lady on the plane. Not me. Alice."

Lady huffed.

"I'm talking to a dog." He shook his head and flipped the meat.

Jack cooked the steak to rare, cut it up, and slid it into a ceramic serving bowl his mom had loaned them to use as Lady's food dish. Lady wolfed it down. After she noisily lapped up half a bowl of water, she pressed against Jack's leg.

He scratched behind her ear. "Are we good now?"

Lady started back down the hallway, and Jack grinned. But just outside the bedroom door, she changed direction and headed into the living room instead.

"Oh, come on. Don't tell me you want to sleep with me now. No way. It's way too hot to be next to a walking space heater covered in fur."

But Lady passed right by Jack's bed. She trotted over to the mantel and looked up at the row of knick-knacks. They included a bright-yellow-and-orange crane standing over a nest of speckled mauve eggs, a tire iron in a glass frame—Jack smiled when he remembered giving that to his father—and, of course, the lime-green découpage sculpture of a fat gecko crouched on its back legs. The statue was twenty inches tall and so wide that the base hung an inch over the edge of the mantel.

Lady let out a long whine.

"Don't be a baby." Jack gave the gecko a little push. "It's fake."

Lady raised her nose, sniffed, and growled.

"It's fake," Jack repeated. He tapped on the large statue for emphasis.

Lady raised herself up on her hind legs, and Jack grabbed her collar. "Whoa, that doesn't mean you get to chew it up like my running shoe." He pulled her back down and rubbed her neck. "Come on. We had a bargain. Back to bed."

Jack had to pull her a couple of times to get her to follow, but he finally managed to convince Lady to return to Alice's room.

Before the door closed, he caught a glimpse of Alice curled up under her sheet, fast asleep. Jack wasn't ready to tell her, but he knew she was right to turn him down. In fact, he had known it from the moment he first asked. The words had just tumbled out of his mouth, and though they had come from the heart—he loved her so much it made his chest ache—in some way, that was exactly the problem.

With love so strong, he was afraid of losing her—like he'd lost Chandler. If war had taught Jack anything, it was weakness. Vulnerability. People wonder why soldiers seem standoffish. Some think it's cocky pride. Maybe for some it is, but for Jack, it was something else.

He knew that at any second Alice could be gone.

He loved her. He'd marry her. But could he open his heart to her, knowing that if something happened to her it would kill him?

Jack returned to the lumpy sofa bed. He was just starting to fall asleep again when his parents' bedroom door opened.

His mother, dressed in a white fluffy bathrobe and carrying an empty glass, quietly shut the door and peeked over at Jack. He waved. She crept to the side of the bed, a worried expression creasing her brow.

"Can you not sleep? Are you too hot? I'm getting your father a glass of water. Would you like one too, honey?"

"No, I'm fine. Thanks, Mom. You're the best."

Her nose wrinkled. "Did you cook steak?"

"For Lady. I'll clean the pan in the morning."

"Don't be silly." She bent down and kissed his head as if he were a child. "Nighty-night."

He listened to her slippers' soft shuffle as she moved into the kitchen. He rolled over and closed his eyes.

A bloodcurdling scream sounded from the kitchen, followed by the sound of breaking glass. From inside Alice's bedroom, Lady let out a string of thunderous barks.

Clothed only in his boxers, Jack sprang out of bed and sprinted toward the kitchen.

His mother stumbled out into the living room, clutching her bathrobe to her chest. Her mouth was moving but no sound was coming out.

"Mom, are you okay?" Jack held her arms and scanned her for injury, but she didn't look hurt.

The sound of a chair sliding across the tile came from the kitchen, followed by the bang of the lanai screen door closing.

Jack's mother grabbed his shoulder with a trembling hand. "There was a man…"

"Lady, get out of the way!" Alice ordered from behind the door.

Ted flung open the bedroom door and rushed toward them.

"Dad, protect Mom!" Jack shouted over Lady's barking. He shoved open the kitchen door. Light gleamed off the broken glass on the tile. The back door was open.

Behind him, Alice's door banged against its frame as Lady pushed against it. He could hear her clawing at the wood and howling.

Ted shouted, "Jack, stop!"

But Jack was already running through the open back door.

Most people run from danger, but not Jack, not now. He ran toward it. He raced into the backyard, toward whoever had dared to enter his parents' home.

The gibbous moon offered enough light for Jack to see that the backyard was empty. He pulled up a mental map of the community. The gate and main road were to the right. He ran that way.

As he dashed across the yard and to the corner of Gladys's house, he forced himself to slow down. The chase had always been the hardest part of being a policeman for him. Part of him loved it so much that the adrenaline coursing through him gave him tunnel vision. He'd focus on only the target and miss the real danger—like the partner of the guy he was chasing. That kind of inattention can get you killed. So he commanded himself to pause.

Jack crept forward, keeping to the shadows and listening for any sound of his prey. The walkway lights that had ringed the pond earlier were now off; they were probably on motion sensors or timers. But light from Gladys's kitchen window spilled into the empty yard.

Behind him, Jack's father ran out of the house. Jack motioned for him to go back in, but Ted headed to the opposite side of the house. A second later, Alice and Lady ran out and followed Ted.

Jack was about to run after all of them when a little dog started yelping in the next house over, past Gladys's. He raced toward the sound, and when he reached the side of the house, he pressed his back against the stucco and listened. The little dog had gone silent.

Jack peered across the yard. Thick bushes, a tall air-conditioning unit, and a car provided plenty of places to hide.

The moon reflected off the still pond. The hot air seemed to thicken as his eyes adjusted to the low light, and he searched the shadows for any movement. He dashed to the next house. The Florida grass was sharp on his bare feet, and surprisingly slick.

The long outdoor patio of this house had a sun cover that blocked the moon's light, making the whole area pitch black. As Jack peered into the darkness, he spotted something moving at the next house over.

"Jack!" his mother called out.

He glanced back and saw his mother awkwardly jogging across the yards, her bathrobe billowing out behind her. Jack was used to hunting monsters, but the thought of his mother anywhere near a thief blasted more intense fear through him than he'd ever felt.

Jack ran back toward her. *"Mom!"* he whispered fiercely. "Go home!" He ran to the edge of the light so she would see him.

The back door to the house behind him opened, and a bright light shined in his face. The old woman in the doorway started to scream. "Police! Police!"

Jack held up his hands. "Lady, I'm the good guy. There's—"

"Don't move, you pervert!" she yelled. "Police! Police!"

Lights started to flick on in every home around the pond.

Jack thought about explaining that she should call 911 rather than shout, "Police!" But from the commotion erupting all over the neighborhood, he was sure someone already had.

He turned to look back at his mother, and pain shot up his legs—as if someone had thrust a needle into his bare foot.

"Jack!"

"Stay back, Laura!" the old woman shouted. "It's a Peeping Tom."

His mother jogged closer. She was panting and looked as though she was about to fall over. "No, he's my son."

More needles stabbed into Jack's feet. He looked down. His feet and ankles looked covered in dirt, but something was wrong—the dirt was moving. And it burned.

"What the hell?" Jack swiped at his feet.

Whatever was on him was biting him. His feet and ankles were covered with what looked like chocolate sprinkles.

"Fire ants!" the old woman called out. "You're on a mound. Wash 'em off, quick!"

Jack sprinted down to the pond. He took two steps into the water and then practically tumbled forward as the bottom of the manmade pond dropped off suddenly. He found himself in water up to his waist. He frantically swiped at the ants, and the ones on his feet floated upward—only to reattach to his thighs and start biting him again.

His hands slapped against his body, and he backed into the pond, splashing as he went. After a minute of flailing about, he thought he'd gotten rid of most of the stinging insects.

"Jack!" His mother waved her arms like a whirligig in a hurricane. "Get out of that pond! Get out right now!"

He stopped splashing. "Calm down, Mom."

"I'd listen to your mother." The old woman shined her light on Jack, and then behind him at the pond. "She's warning you about the gator."

"Gator? In this gated community?" Jack glanced over his shoulder. *I thought Dad was kidding before.*

"Bertha has a nest right near there," the old woman called out.

Bertha?

The light from the old woman's flashlight reflected off the water. A long string of little waves stretched out like contrails from a plane—and it was moving toward Jack. Then something surfaced, and the flashlight reflected off two yellowish eyes.

"Run!" the two women shrieked in unison.

Jack's thighs burned as he pulled his legs through the water and ran for the bank.

"Run!"

Jack reached the shore just as the water behind him erupted in spray. The alligator charged onshore after him. Jack's feet slipped on the slick grass, and he pitched forward. As he fell, he tucked his legs up and rolled away from the alligator.

A roar rose above the women's shrill screams. Lady had bounded forward and landed protectively between Jack and the alligator. She planted her feet and bared her teeth.

Jack scrambled to his feet. He didn't know how a matchup between an alligator and a dog would go, even one as big as Lady, but he wasn't about to let Lady go it alone.

"Back! Back!" he shouted.

The alligator took one look at Lady, twisted around, and slipped back into the pond.

Jack and Lady pressed against each other as they backed up—Lady barking ferociously the whole time. Her entire body trembled against him, and he remembered how scared she was of the geckos.

When they got to the safety of the patio, Jack pulled the enormous dog even closer and wrapped her in a bear hug.

"You have no idea how much I love you, Lady. And I promise you will never have to go on a plane again."

8

SO YOU GOT A BOO-BOO

Curtis Dixon burst through the back door of his aunt's house and shut it fast, his hand leaving a bloody trail down the side of the door. He cradled his bleeding head with his other hand and stomped down the hallway to the bathroom. He grabbed a washcloth and pressed it against the gash in his head, watching the blood drip into the sink. His hand shook with rage as he glared into the mirror.

The hallway light flicked on and footsteps shuffled against the tile.

"You fool!" his aunt hissed as she banged open the bathroom door. "Did anyone see you come here? You woke up the whole—"

"Shut up." Dixon ripped open a cabinet and began yanking out bandages, antiseptic, and gauze. "No one saw me."

"What the hell happened? Did you—"

Dixon slammed the cabinet and stepped nose-to-nose with his aunt. "She surprised me in the kitchen and hit me with a glass."

"And…?" His aunt crossed her arms and glared back.

"Look!" Dixon turned back to the mirror and pointed at a spot two inches above his ear. Light from the vanity gleamed off a shard of glass sticking out of his head.

His aunt stepped up next to him, grabbed the shard, and yanked it out.

Dixon let fly with a stream of curses.

Unfazed, his aunt threw the glass in the trash. "Where's the package?"

Dixon pressed the washcloth against the cut. "I told you. She cut my head!"

"So you got a boo-boo. Put a couple of sissy stickers on it." She grabbed the bandages off the counter and smacked them into his chest. "Where's the package?"

"I didn't get it."

His aunt washed the blood off her hand. "You're telling me that Laura Stratton, who weighs about a buck and a quarter wet, kicked your big bad ass?"

"You didn't tell me other people were there!"

His aunt stared at her reflection in the mirror. Dixon watched as her hard glare softened and her look of refinement returned. "Her son stopped by today. With a girl. I didn't think they were staying overnight."

"You could have given me a heads-up," Dixon snarled as he pulled back the washcloth.

His aunt picked up another washcloth and wet it. She turned Dixon to face her and motioned for him to lower his head. "I apologize for shouting." She dabbed gently at the wound. "The cut isn't that bad. You can't go anywhere right now, though. Things need to cool off. Get cleaned up and I'll figure out how you're going to fix the mess you made tonight. You'll need to go back and get that package."

"I'll get it." Dixon snatched the washcloth out of his aunt's hand, wadded it into a tight ball, and crushed it in his fist. "I'll get it—and then I'm going to make that old broad pay."

9

A FINE-LOOKING BOY

Jack stood in the driveway, dripping wet and clothed only in his boxers. Two cruisers had already arrived, and Jack had brought the policemen up to speed. The police had now fanned out to look for the thief, but had asked Jack to wait there to speak to the senior officer, who was still en route. Old men in bathrobes and old women in hairnets were gathered all around; it looked as if the entire community had gotten up to witness the excitement.

"Everything's fine." Jack held up his hands and tried to calm the crowd. "You should all go home now."

The old woman who had first shouted at Jack from her doorway came out carrying a towel and some medicine for the ant bites. She handed them to Alice. "Here. This will help."

Alice gave Jack the towel, and a smattering of boos rippled from the crowd as he wrapped it around his waist.

Laura's neck rose as she glared. "May I remind you that he's my son."

Ruby stood beside her in a bright-orange robe. "And you raised a fine-looking boy."

Alice sprayed the medicine on Jack's feet. "Boy, those ants might be small, but they have a big bite."

"Speaking of big bites," Ted said, "good thing Lady came along when she did."

"You can say that again." Jack scratched behind Lady's ears. She hadn't left his side since she'd rescued him at the pond.

Laura placed her hand on Jack's back. "That was horrible."

"I don't know about that." Ted winked at Jack. "I thought it was like an old B-movie. *Godzilla vs. the Werewolf.*"

"Lady's a real hero." Alice rubbed the dog's head. "She loves Jack. She was terrified, but she wouldn't let anything happen to him."

"The whole thing was terrifying," Laura said. "I felt helpless."

"Come on, Mom. I've never seen you move that fast!" Jack said.

Ted laughed. "I have. When Jack was seven, he wanted to get Laura's attention. She was at the sink and he was on the stairs." Ted reenacted the action for the crowd of listeners. "He leaned over the railing and waved at her, but she didn't see. So he leaned over further, and poof! He starts falling headfirst."

Ruby gasped.

"The way Laura pounced—it was like watching a *National Geographic* special on lions! She dropped the dish she was cleaning and sprang. Three long strides and she caught Jack by his ankles. It put her back out for a week, but his head never touched the floor."

Color rushed to Jack's cheeks as everyone oohed and aahed.

"You don't remember anything about the guy?" Jack asked his mother again.

She pulled her bathrobe tight and shook her head. "It was so fast. I heard the door, turned to look, and he rushed at me. My hands flew up, and the glass hit him."

"Wow," Ruby said, impressed. "I didn't know you hit him, Laura."

She looked down. "I didn't mean to."

"You did a great job, Mom. Tell me more. Was he wearing a mask? Did you see his hair? Anything?"

She pressed her lips together as tightly as her eyes and stayed like that for a minute. "I'm just not sure. He was a blur. I think he wore jeans, but…"

Jack rubbed her arm. "That's great, Mom. I'll tell the cops that."

Police lights flashed at the end of the block as another cruiser pulled onto the street. A light-blue BMW followed closely behind.

Jack walked forward, wincing on tender feet. He stopped under the streetlight and flagged down the cruiser. As the crowd moved to follow him, Jack turned around. "Okay. Everyone *has* to go back to their homes." A murmur of protest rose. "No one saw anything tonight, so please, go home. Now."

A few of the old folks finally turned and shuffled back toward their homes, but most lingered. *This is probably the most exciting thing that's ever happened in this place,* Jack thought.

The patrol car parked beside Jack, and a policeman in his late fifties opened the door. Because of his pot belly, he had to scoot over before he swung his legs out to get up. As he reached back in for his hat, he kept a puzzled eye on Jack.

The BMW parked behind the cruiser, and Helen Miller, the community manager Jack had met the day before, stepped out.

Jack read the cop's badge. "Evening, Officer French. I'm Jack Stratton. There was a break-in at my parents' house."

Ruby stepped forward. "There've been break-ins all over Orange Blossom. When's something going to be done about it?"

Jack and French were surrounded by the crowd, who all began speaking at once. French held up his hands and asked for quiet, but people just raised their voices even louder.

"Everyone will be heard," Helen said confidently, striding over to stand next to Jack. "I know it's late, but I encourage everyone to accompany me back to the community center so we can discuss this."

Questions flew from the pajama-clad crowd.

"Is it safe?"

"What about the burglar?"

"When is something going to be done?"

"Those are all very good questions, and I'll be happy to answer them all," Helen replied, "but why don't we do it in air conditioning with some snacks? Let's all go back to the community center."

An elderly man raised his hand like a child in class. "Will you have some of those little sugar cookies with the sprinkles?"

Helen nodded. "Tia was putting them out when I left, Mr. Gimble. Now, if you will all follow me, I trust Officer French has everything under control."

French tipped his hat. "I can assure everyone that the situation is under control. We have several patrols out right now and will leave a unit here tonight."

Everyone started talking again.

"But what about tomorrow night?"

"And the rest of the week?"

"Why don't you just catch the guy?"

Helen held up her hands again. "Once we go back to the community center, I'll write down all of these excellent questions for Officer French." To French, she added, "Then, if you'll stop by later, I'll share everyone's concerns with you."

"That's a great idea." French wiped the sweat from his forehead with the back of his sleeve.

Some of the crowd followed Helen, and the rest went back to their homes. Jack walked over to the cruiser with French.

"You chased the guy?" French asked Jack.

Jack nodded. "I was on the job. Sheriff Department in Darrington. I took medical retirement after I got shot." Jack decided to leave out the details of Sheriff Collins forcing him out for disobeying orders.

"Sorry to hear that."

"Life goes on, right?" He gave French the details of the break-in.

"You didn't get any look at him? Even a silhouette?"

"Nothing. By the time I got outside, he was either around a corner or the next yard over. I was following him by noise. My mother saw him, but she was too shaken up by the whole thing to even notice his appearance. She thought he might be wearing jeans."

French tapped his notebook. "Thanks. We'll take it from here."

"People are saying there have been a number of break-ins out here."

"It's all low-level stuff."

"He broke into my parents' home while they were sleeping inside," Jack said. "That's home invasion. It isn't low-level."

"I'm not saying tonight was low-level. I'm saying the past thefts were. With those, no one saw anything, and half the time we couldn't determine if a crime even took place. But don't worry, we take this very seriously. We'll step up patrols."

Jack stuck out his hand. "I appreciate it."

One of the first responding cruisers pulled back onto the street and rolled up. The policeman powered down his window. "Nothing. The guy's a ghost."

Jack glared into the darkness. The intruder had come after his parents.

If he comes back, I'll make him a real ghost.

10

ANIMAL CONTROL

"Jack?" his mother called from the front door. "Did you call animal control?" Jack hurried down the hallway. Standing next to his mother wasn't the uniformed officer he'd expected, but a man around his age, dressed in khaki from head to toe, with shoulder-length, dirty-blond hair pulled back in a ponytail.

"Did you call about the gator?" the man said.

"I did. I'm concerned for my folks and the other residents." Jack peered over the man's shoulder to study the pickup truck parked along the curb. "You're not alone, are you?"

Alice backed into the hallway, keeping Lady in the bedroom as she closed the door behind her.

The man pointed toward the back of the house. "I've got my spotter out at the pond." He thrust out a hand. "Name's Boone."

"Jack. Are you sure you two can get it? You might need more men."

"Ain't too many gators where you need more'n two guys."

"Well, this is one of them," Jack said. "That thing is huge."

"Well, I'll get a lasso, and Bryar an' me'll take a look. Meet you out back."

Alice made a face. "Did he say lasso?"

"Did he say Bryar?" Jack smiled.

As Boone walked to the truck, Laura hugged Jack. "You didn't need to call him."

"What? Mom, it's not like a family of ducks is living in your backyard. It's an alligator that tried to attack a human."

"I don't want them to hurt it."

"Oh, I doubt they will. Unless it tries to hurt *them*."

Jack walked outside as Boone came around the corner holding a long pole with a looped rope on the end.

"Wait!" Alice hurried after them. "What do you do with it when you catch it? You don't kill it, do you?"

"Don't worry." Boone grinned. "I'll take it out to Sunset Swamp Sanctuary. Out there's a gator's paradise. I wish I had it as good as he's gonna have it."

Jack and Alice followed him to the edge of the pond. Another man in a similar outfit but seventy-five pounds heavier waited on the bank.

"That must be Bryar," Jack whispered.

Bryar turned and held up a hand in warning.

Three houses down, Ruby stepped out on her lanai and yelled, "Did you catch it?" Everyone jumped.

Jack held one finger to his mouth, and Ruby waved apologetically.

Bryar pointed at Boone and then to a section of reeds along the bank. The air was completely still and so was the pond, but the reeds moved.

"I'm telling you," Jack warned, "it's big."

"We've got this." Boone jiggled the pole and the lasso shook.

Bryar moved to the right, and Boone headed left. Bryar squatted down near the bank. His head moved on a swivel until he focused on one spot in the reeds. He held up two fingers and pointed.

Boone tapped his chest and crept over to the water's edge. He held the long pole out and let the rope dangle above the water. After a tense wait, he dipped the pole down and yanked up. Water flew into the air as the alligator struggled.

Bryar rushed into the water.

Alice grabbed Jack's arm. "He's crazy."

"I hope they know what they're doing."

Water splashed high into the air. Dark-green scales appeared as Bryar hoisted the alligator out of the water.

"Got it!" Bryar called out.

Boone kept the tension on the lasso, the muscles in his forearms straining as he pulled up on the pole.

Jack and Alice moved back as Bryar walked backward onto the shore.

Bryar turned around with a four-foot alligator wrapped in his arms.

"It's tiny," Alice said.

"That's not the same alligator," Jack protested.

"It's so little!" Alice grinned.

"I've gotta measure it," Boone said, "to make sure it meets state minimum requirements for being a nuisance. Chasing after you and your dog meets one requirement, but it has to be at least four feet. I'm pretty sure it is, but I've got to make sure. Hold on…" He pulled out a measuring tape while Bryar held the alligator against the ground.

"I'm telling you," Jack said, "I saw it. Last night I saw its eyes, and it was a different alligator."

"Maybe you just had a different perspective seeing it at night, down low in the water?" Alice's shoulders trembled, and Jack knew she was trying not to giggle.

"Yeah, I had a meal's-eye view. It tried to eat me."

Alice laughed.

Jack tried to recall any other detail of the alligator. "It only came partway onto the bank, but it looked huge."

"Four feet, one inch!" Boone called out, winding the tape measure. "Just big enough."

"Damn," Jack muttered. He stared at the small alligator and rubbed the back of his neck. "It looked a lot bigger when I was in the water."

"We got a report a week ago that the gator was here," Boone said.

"A week ago? Why didn't you come and get it then?" Jack asked.

"Like I said, it has to meet certain state requirements. This one's small and hadn't bothered nobody."

Bryar wrapped the alligator's mouth closed with tape. When he finished, he wiped his big hands on his large belly. "Cute little guy. And someone's been feedin' him. When I first spotted him, he came right over to me, looking for breakfast."

"It probably wanted *you* for breakfast," Jack said. "It came after me last night."

Bryar scratched at his beard. "You ain't got nothing to worry about with this one. I was tempted to just grab it without the lasso." He wrapped the alligator's lower body in a tarp.

"Thanks for calling us." Boone shook Jack's hand and then followed Bryar as he carried the alligator to the truck.

Jack turned to Alice. He could tell she was still trying to suppress a giggle, so he quickly changed the subject. "Do you mind giving me a hand with something before I go out with my dad?"

"Sure. What?"

"My parents' alarm system. I want to make sure everything's secure and they know how to arm it."

11

TWO BY FOUR

Jack stopped at the exit of the complex. "Where do you want to go?" he asked his father.

"Take a left." A mischievous grin spread across Ted's face. "I'm starving. I missed lunch."

"Where are we going?"

Ted's smile widened even further. "Coffee. I told your mom that you and I were going out to grab a coffee and have a talk. Are you hungry?"

"I thought you're on a diet."

Ted looked over his shoulder as if Laura could hear him. "I am. But if your mother asks, just tell her we went for coffee."

"I'm not going to lie to Mom."

"I'm not telling you to lie. We'll get coffee. You just don't have to give your mother a summary of what I eat."

Ted gave Jack directions, and ten minutes later they parked in front of a little brick building with an enormous yellow sign.

"The Waffle Palace?" Jack said. "If you want something to eat, Dad, I'll take you someplace that has some healthier options—my treat."

"No thanks. Everyone from Orange Blossom Cove loves this place. They've given it five gold forks. I've been dying to try it, and your mother keeps saying *soon, we'll go soon*. She hopes I'll forget about it. But soon is now! This is great! We'll get our coffee...and some eggs and bacon, too." Ted rubbed his hands together like a little kid about to get dessert.

"Dad...I told you. I'm not lying to Mom."

"Of course not. Just don't say I ate anything. This diet she has me on is killing me, and I haven't so much as cheated with a Tic Tac. I'm due." He got out of the car. "Besides, you said you had something you wanted to talk about."

Jack clicked his tongue. He did want his father's advice, and he'd been waiting for the right time.

Looks like this is it. Soon is now.

The waitress showed them to a corner booth. Ted waved off the menu. "I know what I'd like. I'll have the two by four."

"Two pancakes, two eggs, two sausages, and two bacon?"

"Yes, please."

Jack shook his head. "You'd better hope Mom doesn't ask me." He handed his menu to the waitress. "I'll have a Western omelet and a sweet tea, please."

Ted said a quick grace, put his napkin on his lap, and picked up his fork.

Jack laughed. "Dad, you look like you've been on a desert island and haven't seen food in a year."

"That's what I feel like. Your mother makes those personal trainers on TV look like teddy bears. She's ruthless. She has all these programs on my phone that monitor everything I eat." He held up his arm and tapped a band around his wrist. "It's like I've been abducted by an alien fat farm. This electronic leash monitors every step I take and what cardiac zone I hit. It even tracks my sleep."

Jack chuckled. "Now you know how I felt at seventeen."

"It's not funny."

"Dad, it's just a fitness monitor. I told her to get you one."

His father leveled his fork at him. "This is *your* fault?"

"We're just trying to help."

"Are you the one who told her about that smart water bottle?"

Jack grinned. "You never drink water."

"Did you know that stupid bottle sends a picture of a cute little plant to your mother's phone? If I don't drink enough water, the plant makes a frowny face, your mother feels bad, and she has me drinking like a camel until the plant's smiling again. Then I make four to six trips to the bathroom in the next three hours."

"We just care about you, Dad."

"I know, and I love you for it. But I've dreamt about pancakes, bacon, and eggs for the last two weeks. I even stuck to the diet on the cruise. Try going by a buffet every day and not touching a thing. It's not easy. One meal under the radar is not going to blow a diet. If I don't get some grease in me, *I'm* going to sprout leaves."

Jack coughed to cover a laugh.

"So." Ted set his fork down. "What did you want to talk to me about?"

Jack shifted in his seat. "Alice. I asked her to marry me."

Ted took off his glasses and started to clean them. "Okay... This was not unexpected. Aunt Haddie tipped us off that you two were heading that way. I assume she said yes?"

"Well..." Jack cleared his throat. "I kinda assumed that she'd say yes, too. That's why I asked her. But...she said no."

"She said no?"

"Well, not exactly no."

Ted put his glasses back on and steepled his hands with his elbows on the table. "I'm not following. It's a yes-or-no question, Jack. What was her answer?"

"'Not right now.' But she said no because she said I should do it right."

"Do it right?" Ted repeated. "How exactly did you do it wrong?"

Jack shrugged. "I don't know. I just asked. You know?"

Ted cocked an eyebrow. "You've got to give me a little more to go on. Let's start with the where. Where did you ask her?"

Jack fanned his hand out to the restaurant. "It was a place like this. Do you know that breakfast spot on Washington Street in Darrington? The Sunrise Cafe?"

"I know it. I used to take your mother there. Did you meet Alice there?"

"No."

"Does Sunrise Cafe hold some special connection for you two?"

"No. We were having breakfast, and I realized she's the one."

Ted pressed his hands down on the table and leaned in. "Please don't tell me your proposal was something like, 'How's your pancake? Oh, by the way, do you want to get married?' Was it?"

Jack sat back. "I was in the moment."

"You didn't just say that."

"I thought she would think it was spontaneous and romantic."

"Women love romantic and spontaneous when you pick them up flowers or make dinner reservations. When you're talking about a lifetime commitment, they want a little thought and planning to go into it. They want you to make it extra-special, too."

Jack's broad shoulders slumped. "That's kinda what Alice said." He picked up a sugar packet. "She was a little more animated about it, though."

The waitress brought over a coffee and a sweet tea. Ted gleefully added sugar and cream to his coffee.

"Dad?"

Ted held up a hand and took a sip of his coffee. A little smile spread across his face. "Sorry. I've been having it black and forgot how good a little sugar and cream can taste."

"I'm kinda freaking out here and looking for your advice, Dad. Can you focus on your beloved son instead of your coffee, please?"

"Relax. You've got no reason to panic. She didn't say no to marrying you. She just shot down your proposal. She also gave you sound advice. The first question you need to ask yourself, Jack, is if you're ready to get married."

"I thought the first question is, 'Do I love her?'"

Ted took another sip and set the cup down. "You've already answered that one. Anyone can take one look at the two of you together and there's no doubt about that. I'm talking about you being responsible."

The waitress brought over their food. While they ate, Ted ran down a list of questions he had for Jack.

When Ted had one forkful left, he paused. "Hold on, Jack." He gazed down at the fork. It had a piece of sausage skewered over a bit of pancake, and the last chunk of scrambled eggs sprinkled with bacon was on the ends of the tines. He closed his eyes and savored the bite.

"I'll bring you back tomorrow if you want, Dad."

His father shook his head. "No. I might complain about all your mother's NSA-type monitoring of my dietary habits," he grinned, "but I want to stick around a little longer for her." He set his fork down on the plate. "Okay, back to you. You want to talk about love. It's as sweet as maple syrup…"

"Come on, Dad! I will never try to have a serious conversation with you in a breakfast joint ever again."

"This coming from a guy who just proposed in one."

"Touché."

Ted continued. "As far as marriage goes, it looks like you've got all your bases covered except one."

"What one?"

"Are you two really ready? It's a lifetime commitment. It's a giant step you have to take together and keep on taking together every day. If one of you isn't ready, it won't work in the long run. You're at a crossroads, Jack. You need to take time and do some soul searching. Be completely honest with yourselves and with each other. You need to ask yourself what's right for Jack before you can truly commit yourself to Alice. And Alice needs to do the same thing. That's what I meant about you being responsible. Marriage is a huge responsibility, and when it's done right, it really is as sweet as maple syrup."

"Thanks, Dad." Jack slid the glass of water closer to his dad's hand. "Now take a long sip and make sure that plant won't be frowning when we get back."

12

THE BATTLE BUTTERFLY

J ack hung up his phone as he took the exit off the highway. "Do you mind if we make another stop, Dad?"

"Not at all. Where?"

"You know how I've been trying to find anyone who knew Alice's family? I think I found her—that's who just called me. Her name is Amanda Holt. She was a friend of Alice's mother and said we could swing by. She's over in Kissimmee."

"I never realized Alice didn't have anything to remember her family by."

"Her parents had no relatives and no will. After they died, Alice got placed in foster care." Jack stopped at the traffic light. "This lady is my last hope."

***

"I really appreciate you meeting me, Amanda." Jack sat on a white sofa in a modest living room. His father sat next to him.

"I couldn't believe it when you called. I always wondered what happened to little Alice. It was so sad about the Campbells."

"Did you know the family well?" Jack asked.

"We were neighbors, and Ally and I were best friends."

"Ally?" Jack repeated.

"Alice was named after her mother, so we called her mother Ally, and Alice was 'little Alice.' I was going through the end of my marriage, and whenever Ally was in town, she was my shoulder to cry on."

"In town? Was she away often?"

"All the time. Work, mostly."

"I thought Alice's parents owned a floral shop," Jack said.

"Alice's father, Chris, ran it. Ally did some consulting work, so she traveled. Internationally." Amanda said this with a mix of pride and awe. "But you couldn't have asked for a better friend or mother. She really doted on those kids."

"That's why I tracked you down. I was hoping you might have a picture, anything…"

"Well, to be honest, after my divorce, I followed Cortez's example."

"The explorer?" Ted asked.

"Cortez burned his boats so there was no going back." Amanda lifted her chin and sighed. "That's what I did with most of my things after the divorce. I threw them all out."

Jack put his elbows on his knees and leaned forward. "You got rid of everything?"

"Well. Not *everything*." Amanda turned to the end table, picked up a cardboard box, and placed it on the coffee table. "I dug through my storage closet and found a couple of things you might be interested in." She took out a framed photo. "I took this during our Fourth of July barbecue. I thought little Alice should have this."

Jack had to stop himself from snatching the photo from her hand. It was a picture of Alice's entire family. Her father had one arm wrapped around her mother and the other around Alice's shoulders. Climbing on her father's shoulders were her two younger brothers. They were twins.

Her father had short brown hair and emerald-green eyes. Jack was surprised to see that his wife was taller than he was. Alice's mother was striking, and even in the picture she presented a grace of movement. Her skin was a light bronze, and there was something about her high cheekbones and sharp features that made Jack want to try to place her nationality, but he couldn't. Her long, deep-brown hair was pulled back in a ponytail slipped through a baseball cap.

"Ally was just gorgeous." Amanda's fingertip gently touched the glass. "She was beautiful inside and out. And these are Alice's brothers, Andrew and Alex. They were six." The twins were identical right down to their dirty-blond hair, huge grins, and missing front teeth.

"How is little Alice?" Amanda asked. "She was only seven then. She must be a grown woman now."

"She's great. I'm sure she'd love to talk to you. But I actually haven't told her yet that I'm looking for this. I hit so many dead ends trying to find anyone who knew the Campbells, and I didn't want to get her hopes up."

"Well, if she wants to, I would love to hear from her." Amanda turned back to the box. "There's one more thing I found. Ally gave it to me." She removed a small jewelry box and held it out like a child presenting a surprise. "Ally's wearing it in the photo. I've treasured this gift from my dear friend, but little Alice should really have it."

She opened the box, revealing a delicate silver-and-blue butterfly brooch. Jack looked back at the photo and saw the same brooch pinned on Ally's chest.

"Ally gave it to me at the barbecue. I had just gotten into another fight with my ex, and Ally…she just took it off and pinned it on me. She called it her 'battle butterfly,' and told me to wear it until I was through the worst of it. It was supposed to be a reminder that things were going to change and get better. Ally loved butterflies. Anyway, she made me believe that I could still have a life. Beautiful and strong, like the butterfly." Amanda wiped away a tear. "She was like that. She'd give you the shirt off her back if you needed it. Would you please give it to little Alice?"

"Alice will be… You have no idea what this will mean to her." Jack cradled the box in his palm.

"I really would love to talk to her. I'm heading up north at the end of the month. My sister is retiring, so I'm going to spend two weeks in Darrington." She scribbled her name, a phone number, and an email address on a notepad. "Just let me know."

"I will."

"It was nice meeting you," Ted said.

"You too." She turned to Jack. "Do you know if they ever caught the driver of the truck who killed them?"

"I thought the other driver fell asleep and was killed in the accident."

"No. The truck was stolen. The other driver fled the scene. They never caught him."

***

As they walked back to the car, Ted looked over at his son. "Are you okay?"

Jack slipped behind the wheel and put the jewelry box and photo in the glove compartment. "Alice never mentioned her mother working—let alone her traveling out of the country."

"She was young when she lost them. Kids remember things differently."

"Yeah, that's the problem," Jack said.

"What do you mean?"

"I mean, the car accident. How do I tell her she has something like that wrong? She thinks the other driver died. How do I tell her they never caught the guy who killed her family?"

Ted took off his glasses and began to clean them. After a moment, he cleared his throat. "Very tactfully. That's going to be a tough pill to swallow."

"Yeah." Jack pulled the car away from the curb. "I think she's going to need that battle butterfly."

13

A BAD IDEA

Alice sat at the kitchen table, waiting for Jack's mother. Jack planned to go out with his father that evening, so Laura had suggested they have a girls' night. Alice was expecting to watch *Wheel of Fortune*, bake a pie, or go through more photo albums. So when Laura came in wearing dark sweatpants and a black T-shirt, Alice was thrown off.

Laura looked at Alice's summer outfit and frowned. "You might want to change."

"Okay. What're we doing tonight?"

The doorbell rang. "Oh, good. They're early. One second."

Laura went down the hall, and Alice followed.

Ellie, Ginny, and Ruby marched in. They were all dressed in black too. They exchanged excited grins.

Ruby looked Alice up and down and bit her lower lip. "Look at you."

"You're in all white," Ginny said.

"You glow," Ellie added, "and not in a good way."

All four women shook their heads in sync. Ruby spoke for the group. "You need to change, sugar. You'll stick out like a Roman candle at midnight."

"Um, where are we going?" Alice asked.

The four women exchanged impish winks.

"Just pick out something dark," Ginny instructed.

"If you have to have a dash of color, be sure it's muted and understated." Ruby touched a dark-purple brooch fixed to her black turtleneck.

"I'll be right back." Alice hurried into her bedroom.

Lady lifted her head off the bed as she entered.

"This is one girls' night I have a feeling you're lucky to miss, Lady." Alice pulled on some black leggings, but the only dark T-shirt she'd packed was a dark-blue one with HOPE FALLS across the front in big gold letters. She put it on.

When she stepped out of the bedroom, the women from the book club all frowned.

"Can you turn it inside out?" Laura suggested.

"Uh, won't that look a little odd?" Alice eyed each woman, trying to understand.

"It's just us, darling." Ruby nodded wisely. "It'll be fine."

Alice darted back into the room and turned the T-shirt inside out. The letters felt scratchy against her soft skin. "I wonder if this is some kind of weird test?" she whispered to Lady. She patted Lady's head before she walked back into the hallway.

"Looks like we're ready," Ginny declared.

"Let's get this party started!" Ellie took Alice by the hand, and the five formed a line out the door.

A green Prius was parked in the driveway. Ginny got in the driver's seat, Laura in the passenger seat, and Ruby and Ellie sat on both sides of Alice in the back.

Laura snapped on her seat belt. "Head over to the Swansons'."

"The Swansons'?" Ginny repeated. "Oh, that's right. They're in Ohio for their son's wedding."

Ginny put her blinker on and took a right out of the driveway. She drove slowly around the complex to a cul-de-sac.

"Park in the McMillens' driveway," Laura said. "They're still up in New Hampshire."

Ginny pulled into a driveway and turned off the headlights, but left the car running.

Alice looked at the women dressed in all black, and her eyes widened. "Wait a second. You're not the ones stealing stuff, are you?"

The three older women looked first at Laura, then at each other, and then back at Alice.

"Us?" Ruby said.

"Thieves?" Ginny said.

"Oh, no." Ellie shook her head.

All four women broke into fits of laughter. Ruby laughed so hard the little car rocked back and forth.

Alice unlatched her seat belt and waved her hands. "Okay, go ahead and snicker and be mysterious all you want, but why else are we parked in a deserted driveway, dressed all in black, watching a house where the people are away? Unless you're planning to…" It suddenly hit her. "Wait. Are we on a stakeout?"

"She got it!" Ginny smiled.

Ruby gave her a thumbs-up, and Ellie clapped.

Laura sat up straight. "Whoever's been stealing things from people's homes crossed a line last night. They came into my home with my son sleeping in the living room. I'm not going to just sit back and do nothing."

A knot formed in Alice's stomach. "Ah, I think we should talk to Jack about this."

Laura shook her head. "I did. I spoke to his father, too. But some things fall to the women of the house. And this is one of those things. We're the protectors."

"Like a lioness protecting the pride." Ginny made a clawing motion with her hand for emphasis.

Alice tried to look back at the Swansons' house, but it was hard to turn when she was being squished in the tiny backseat between Ruby and Ellie.

"Why didn't you back into the driveway?" Ruby complained.

"I wanted to look inconspicuous," said Ginny.

"Can you turn the car around?" Ellie asked.

Ginny pointed. "Just look in the mirrors."

"We don't have mirrors back here," Ruby countered.

Alice looked out the window at the glow of a streetlight forming a soft circle a few yards from the driveway. "I still think we should run it by Jack."

"There are times in your life when you run things by your husband, and times you don't," Ruby said.

"Stakeouts are a *don't* time," Ellie added.

"How would you know?" Ginny shot back. "You've never been on one."

"And neither have you."

"None of us have," Ruby said.

"I have," Alice said.

Ruby rolled her eyes.

"I have!" Alice said defensively.

"Shhh…" Laura waved her hands for everyone to quiet down.

"What? It's too soon for anything to happen," Ruby said.

"We just got here," Ellie agreed.

"We should have brought some snacks." Ruby rummaged through her purse. "Maybe I have some gum."

"Oh!" Ginny slapped her knee. "I forgot my sweet tea. All I have is this watered-down old Sprite." She reached over to the cup holder and sipped from an extra-large fast-food cup.

"Shhh…" Laura was louder now. She pointed. "Look."

Alice peered over Ellie's shoulder. In the back of the house, a little beam of light danced across the yard.

Laura opened her door, and the rest of the women followed suit.

"Um, I'm going to call the police." Alice reached into her pocket for her phone, only to realize it was still on the Strattons' kitchen table. "I don't have it on me. Who's got a phone?"

All four women shook their heads.

"We can't call the police until we're sure anyway." Laura quietly closed her door. "Let's go get a look."

"Bad idea." Alice shut her door just as quietly. "Trust me. This is not a good idea."

Two other doors clicked closed, and they all hurried across the street. Laura moved to the corner of the house and stopped, leaning against the stucco.

Alice tried to peer around the back of the house. *Jack is going to kill me for this. I should have talked sense into these ladies. They should know better!*

As they stood in the shadow of the house, considering their next move, Ginny's car's headlights flashed, and a loud electronic beep caused everyone except Ginny to hop in the air.

"Sorry," Ginny whispered. "I forgot to lock it."

Ruby looked as though she were about to let Ginny have it, but instead she held up her finger and pressed it to her lips.

"I don't see the light anymore," Ellie whispered.

"Maybe the car scared them off," Ruby grumbled. She glared at Ginny, who scrunched up her face.

"You're right. They're gone. We should go." Alice jerked her thumb back toward the car.

"Wait." Laura held up her hand. "Listen."

The women clumped together, one giant mass of black, and strained to hear any sound out of the ordinary. And then, behind the house, the little light clicked on again. It swept briefly across the yard before it clicked off once more.

"Someone's in the house." Ellie's voice trembled.

"I think they're in the backyard," Alice said.

"No, they're in the house," Ruby said. "The light is shining out through the back window."

Ellie nodded.

"What do we do?" Ginny asked.

"Let's go call the police," Alice suggested.

"But we can catch them red-handed," Laura whispered.

"No." Alice shook her head. "That's a really, really bad idea."

"Come on." Laura moved toward the front door.

"How are you going to get in?" Ellie asked.

"Mary keeps a hide-a-key in that fake rock next to the front steps." Ginny picked up the rock and took out the key.

"Mrs. Stratton," Alice whispered, "this is not safe. Really not safe. He may have a gun."

"It's Mr. Hubbard, I'm sure of it," Ruby said. "He ate my brownie right off my napkin once at bingo. That is theft. And he doesn't have a gun."

"It is not Mr. Hubbard," Ginny said. "It's Flo. I saw the way she kept looking at Mary's china set. She even offered to buy it. Flo is in there right now taking it!"

"Shhhh. It isn't either of them," Ellie whispered. "I know it's—"

Alice rushed in front of the women and planted herself directly in front of the door. "You could all be wrong. It could be a *real* bad guy. This isn't a game. I can't let you do this." She set her feet shoulder-width apart and held her arms out.

Ginny faked left and Ruby darted right. Ruby slipped behind Alice, opened the door, and slipped inside. Ginny, Ellie, and Laura followed.

"No, no, no, Mrs. Stratton." Alice hurried after them.

When Ginny shut the door behind them, they were plunged into complete darkness. Drawn shades kept out all but little slivers of light from the streetlights outside.

"I'll call the police," Alice whispered. "Where's the phone?"

"Boy, for someone who says they've been on a stakeout, you sure have your panties in a bunch," Ruby said.

Laura nudged Ruby and Alice. "You're both far too noisy. Shh."

The group made their way down the hallway, feeling along the wall as they went. Laura slowly opened the door to the kitchen. It appeared empty.

"I can't see anything," Ellie whispered.

Alice sighed. "If anyone was in here, they already know we're coming...unless they're deaf."

"Mr. Kendric's almost deaf," Ellie said. "That's who's got my vote. He's an ex-cop. He knows how to disable security."

Security systems... Oh, no.

"Mrs. Stratton! Did someone shut off the alarm to the house?"

"Mr. Kendric must have disabled it!" Ellie's fist pounded into her palm. "I knew it."

"Mary never turns it on," Ginny said. "I water their plants. I know."

"Shhh..." Laura whispered. Something in her hand flashed, blinding everyone.

"Laura!" Ruby snapped.

"Sorry," Laura grumbled. "My phone's got a flashlight app. I just don't know how to use it. That was the camera."

Alice put her hands on her hips. "You *do* have a phone."

Laura smiled sheepishly. "Oops."

Alice exhaled. She never imagined she'd be the responsible one in *this* group.

"I can't see at all now. Just spots." Ellie rubbed her eyes.

"Just…keep your eyes closed," Ginny advised.

Alice covered her mouth. They were making so much noise, if there really was a real thief, he would be long gone by now—she hoped. But she had another problem. She was starting to fight a losing battle with a case of the giggles, and the last thing she wanted was for Jack's mother to think she was laughing at them.

Flashing blue lights streamed in through the front windows as a car skidded to a stop out on the road.

The women all turned to stare at Laura. She rushed over to the back window, opened it, and pointed at Alice. "Go."

"I can't leave you."

"We'll come right after you. Go!" Laura grabbed Alice's shoulder and pulled her toward the opening.

The front door banged open. "This is the police!" a voice yelled. "Come out of the house now with your hands over your head!"

Alice dove out the window. As she rolled to her feet, Laura closed the window.

"What are you doing?" Alice mouthed.

Laura mouthed the word "run." She even wiggled two fingers, charade-like.

Alice crouched low and sprinted away, sticking to the shadows.

"Come out of the house with your hands above your head!" the policeman shouted again.

Two more cruisers raced down the street with their lights and sirens flashing.

"No, no, no," Alice repeated as she circled around the house.

The two cruisers stopped in front of Ginny's car, and while one policeman hopped out and joined the first officer, another trained a spotlight on the front door.

Alice slipped into the gathering crowd.

"You in the house!" one of the policemen bellowed into a bullhorn. "Come out with your hands over your head!"

Alice's breath came in rapid little puffs as Laura appeared at the doorway with her hands over her head.

No, no, no… How am I going to tell Jack that his mom just got arrested?

14

_____

I'D LIKE TO JOIN

"**D**id you like your *coffee*, Jack?" Ted parked the car in the driveway. Jack laughed. "You'd better take some acting lessons before you try that line in front of Mom."

"That was *good*. It was natural. Wasn't it?"

Jack climbed out of the car, smiling and shaking his head. "I think you've lost your acting touch since the talent show, Dad. You can honestly say that you stuck to your diet for lunch and dinner. That's the truth. We won't even bring up breakfast. Now I'm going to walk Lady while you go inside, change, and throw on some sneakers. We'll go to the gym in the community center when I get back."

"You're kidding, right?" Ted closed his door.

"You have to work off those pancakes."

"But it's father-son night."

"And I want many more of them," Jack said. "We can talk on the treadmill."

Ted sighed. "You're right. Besides, I'm no good at keeping secrets from your mother."

"You need to change your shirt anyway. You left a little pancake evidence."

"What?" Ted looked down at a spot of dried syrup on his shirt. "Well, no wonder I'm no good at keeping secrets."

***

When Jack and Lady returned from their walk, an ivory BMW had just parked in the driveway. A tall, chic woman with silver shoulder-length hair eased out of the driver's side and walked straight up to Jack.

Lady strained at the leash, and the woman held out a graceful hand for the dog to get her scent. Jack smelled the lilac, too. Lady's thick tail wagged and the woman gave her a light pat.

"What a magnificent animal." She shook Jack's hand firmly. "You must be Jack. I'm Janet Ferguson. It's nice to meet you. I'm here to see your mother."

"I'm sorry, but my mother is out with my girlfriend. Is there something my father can help you with?"

"I believe he can. Thank you." She tucked her white Prada handbag under her arm. Jack couldn't help but notice how perfectly the color of the bag with its gold clasp matched her expensive-looking high heels and embroidered linen tunic. Everything about her said opulence.

Jack led her inside and put Lady into the bedroom before he returned. "Can I offer you a drink?"

Janet's smile was disarming. Jack felt himself shifting awkwardly from one foot to another. This woman seemed in a class well above his usual social circles. "No, thank you. I won't be keeping you long." She strolled into the living room, her eyes traveling all over like a real estate agent appraising a new property.

Ted walked out of the bedroom dressed in gym shorts and sneakers. He had no shirt on, as he was carrying his T-shirt in his hand. When he saw Janet, he darted back behind the cover of the door.

"Hello, Ted." Janet's lips curled up into a tight smile. "My apologies for stopping by unannounced."

Ted reappeared, red-faced, wearing his shirt this time. "You're always welcome, Janet. It's not your fault that no one told me you were here." He shot a stern look at Jack.

"I didn't make you—" Jack started to say, but the continuing glare from his father made him think better of what he was about to say.

"Nice of you to come by, Janet," Ted said. "I'm sorry, but Laura's not here."

"Your son informed me." She turned to look at Jack. "I am parched. Would it be any trouble to have that drink you so kindly offered, dear?"

"Of course. We have, uh, coffee, sweet tea, juice, water…"

"An ice water would be lovely, thank you." She looked at Ted and held out a hand to the couch. "May I?"

"Certainly." Ted smiled, but Jack picked up on the tightening around his blue eyes. *This lady makes Dad uncomfortable too.*

"I'll be right back." Jack went to the kitchen and poured two glasses of ice water. He returned and handed one to his father, who had sat in the club chair next to the couch, and the other to Janet.

"Thank you." Janet crossed her long legs. Her tan linen skirt had a slit in it that now exposed a good deal of her toned thigh.

If a retirement community ever had a poster girl, Jack thought, *Janet Ferguson would win hands down.* She exuded a polished elegance, with model good looks and the magnetism of a movie star. The water droplets forming on her glass passed over her slender fingers.

"Well, I don't want to delay your workout," Janet said, "so I'll try to get right to the point. I'd like to spend some time with you." She set down her glass on a coaster; the slight bump didn't cover the sound of Ted gulping at her words. "And the book club," she added.

Ted took off his glasses and started cleaning the lenses. "I beg your pardon?"

Janet glided over to the end of the couch and leaned in closer to Ted. "An old Chinese proverb says a book is like a garden carried in a pocket. I'm not terribly fond of getting my hands dirty, but I do like flowers. I thought the offer to join the book club was open to all Orange Blossom residents."

Ted cleared his throat and put his glasses back on. "Yes, of course. I'm sure they'll be glad to have you join them."

"Them?"

"My wife and the other members."

"You're not a member of the club, Ted? Don't you find pleasure in books?"

"I do. I mean, no, I'm not a member but I do find pleas—I like to read."

Janet set her elbow on the edge of the couch and cradled her chin in her palm. She stared at Ted as if studying a painting. "And what do you enjoy reading?"

"Thrillers. Mostly. And—"

Jack's ears perked up. Police sirens wailed in the distance, and they sounded as if they were coming closer. Lady started to bark.

"I wonder if there's been another break-in?" Ted hopped up, hurried to the window, and peered out.

Police lights flashed on the trees as a cruiser sped down the street.

Janet stood. "That's a frightening thought."

"I'm sure the police will handle it," Ted said reassuringly.

"Of course." Janet picked up her bag. "They're the ones with guns, after all. But I do need to be going. I've taken up far too much of your time."

"Not at all. I'll let Laura know that you stopped by. She will be sorry she missed you." Ted followed Janet to the door.

"Thank you, Ted. Please do. And if it's not too much trouble, would you be a dear and drop off the book the club is reading? *You* can bring it by *any time.*"

Ted opened his mouth, promptly closed it, and nodded.

Janet gave Jack a delicate wave and sauntered back to her ivory BMW as another cruiser raced down the street.

15

JUMPING TO CONCLUSIONS

"I'm going to take Lady and check out where the police went," Jack said. "I'll go with you."

Jack turned to go, but Ted grabbed his arm. "Wait a second. Alice is heading this way."

Jack looked out the window. Alice raced down the sidewalk at full speed. When Jack realized that she was running away from the direction the police had gone, his stomach tightened.

Out of breath and gasping for air, Alice slowed to a stop on the walkway. She raised one hand in an awkward wave. "Hi."

Jack pointed. "Your shirt's on inside out."

Alice's lips pulled back into an I'm-so-sorry-that-I-have-to-tell-you-this smile.

"What did you do?" Jack said.

"Nothing. I didn't do anything."

"Alice…"

Ted raised a cautioning hand. "Now, Jack, don't go leaping to any conclusions. I'm sure everything's okay."

"Thanks, Mr. Stratton." Alice shifted her weight from foot to foot. "But I tried to tell her no. I really, really did."

Ted turned to look at Jack, who smiled and said, "Don't go jumping to any conclusions, Dad."

"Mrs. Stratton…" Alice said. "Well, she thought… See, I was like, 'This is a bad idea,' but none of them would listen. I tried to tell them, but… And who makes a fake rock to put a key in? And they were all dressed in black. I should have known something was up, but it was supposed to be a girls' night—"

"Alice…" Ted put his hands on her shoulders. "Breathe. Deep breaths."

Alice gulped in air.

"Now, what happened?"

Alice winced. "Your wife got arrested."

***

Jack and his father both paced the floor at the police station, going in opposite directions. Alice leaned against the wall, nervously tapping her foot. Every once in a while, either Jack or his father would throw his hands up and glare at the ceiling. Each time, Alice winced and grimaced.

Finally, the door behind the desk opened, and Officer French walked out. He didn't look happy.

"Mr. Stratton."

Both men replied at the same time. "Yes?"

"We're releasing Ellie Harper, Ginny Peek, and Ruby Green."

"But what about my wife?" Ted asked.

"She's being charged," French stated flatly.

"Charged?" Ted and Jack both stepped forward.

"I spoke with Hank Swanson," Ted explained. "He's the homeowner. He said he's not pressing charges. He's a family friend. The covering desk sergeant spoke with him, too."

"She's not being charged with breaking and entering," French said.

"Then what could you charge her with?" Jack asked.

"Resisting arrest." French folded his hands in front of himself.

"Resist—what?" Jack asked incredulously. "My *mother*?"

"I tried to frisk her, and she caused an over-the-top spectacle. She made a number of allegations against me personally, too." The color rose in French's neck.

"Can I talk to her?" Jack asked.

French thought for a moment. "She hasn't been processed. I'll give you five minutes. She's in there."

French led Jack and his father into the interrogation room. Alice started to follow, but with one sideways glance from Jack, she stayed where she was.

Laura Stratton sat behind a metal table with her hands demurely folded in her lap. "Are they letting me go now?"

Both Ted and Jack crossed their arms. Ted opened his mouth to speak, but Jack spoke first. "Mom, Officer French said you resisted arrest. Please tell me he's got you confused with someone else."

"Don't be silly, Jack. Of course I didn't resist arrest."

Jack exhaled.

Ted chuckled. "I knew there had to have been some mistake."

"I just refused to let him touch me. It was completely inappropriate."

Jack did a double take. "You what?"

Laura sat up straighter. "You should have seen the way he touched Ellie. One second he told her to put her arms out, and the next thing you know, his hands are traveling all over her. And I mean *all over* her body."

"Mom…" Jack tapped the metal table. "You're describing getting frisked. Did he grope or linger or do anything that was unprofessional?"

Laura made a sour face. "The others may have thought it was okay, but I wasn't about to let him touch me in that manner."

Jack looked at his father, but Ted just shrugged. Jack's frustration rose. "Mom, was this cop just doing his job? I have to frisk people all the time."

"But those are criminals," Laura explained. "I pay my taxes and I haven't done anything wrong. I am a married woman. No one but your father touches me."

Jack shook his head. "French thought you broke into a house."

"But I didn't. Ginny knew where Mary kept the key."

"It's still B&E because Mary didn't give you permission to enter, Mom," Jack snapped.

"I don't care for your tone, young man."

"All I'm asking is whether this cop crossed a line." His mother started to protest, but Jack held up a hand to cut her off. "Say a *bad* lady had broken into that house. If the cop frisked her the way he frisked Ellie, would he have been doing it in an unprofessional way?"

Laura thought for a moment. "No. But it would still have been more appropriate if a female officer did the frisking. I told him that."

French knocked at the door and opened it up. "Time."

Laura started to stand, but French shook his head. "She stays."

Jack walked to the door. "Officer French, may I speak with you a moment?"

French held the door open, and Jack stepped out.

"I want to apologize for my mother," Jack began.

"Well, she was making some pretty serious accusations. You know…inappropriate touching, and…" he looked uncomfortable, "and things like that."

"She didn't mean that you were touching anyone inappropriately," Jack said. "I can assure you of that."

"Well, it sure sounded like it." French tugged his belt a little higher. "And I *had* to frisk them. I mean, I know their age, but we have procedures to follow. I'd be in trouble if I *didn't* frisk them."

"I completely understand. It's just my mom wanted a female officer—"

"She never requested that. She didn't."

Jack saw the opening he was looking for. "She didn't formally request it, but she did say she thought a female officer would be more appropriate."

"But she didn't request one."

"Can you see where the communication got muddled? It happens. Look, I would consider it a huge personal favor if you could reconsider this."

"But what if one of these ladies decides to complain later? I need to protect myself. I didn't do anything inappropriate."

"I know that. You know that, and my mother knows that. I'll even have her sign something to that effect."

French scratched at his jaw. "You're on the job. You know how it is."

"I do. And I agree with you. Just give me one more second to talk to her."

Jack went back into the interrogation room. Ted stood behind Laura, with his hand on her shoulder.

"Okay. I got him to drop the charges as long as Mom apologizes and agrees to sign a paper saying he didn't do anything inappropriate."

"I will do no such thing," Laura said.

Jack shook his head. "No. You will do *exactly* such a thing. You're wrong on this, Mom. That guy was just doing his job."

Laura crossed her arms. "I don't think it was appropriate."

"I'm not going to argue with you, but I am going to say two things. One, you should have asked for a female officer right then. Two, jail is not a fun place."

Laura glared. "Fine. If you agree to help me find the real thief, then I'll apologize."

"You don't get to bargain, Mom. Your bargain is staying out of jail."

French knocked on the door again.

Jack huffed. "We'll talk about it at home. Just say you're sorry, Mom."

French stepped into the room, and Laura stood. "Officer French, my son has made it clear to me that I owe you an apology."

16

NO PRESSURE

"I still think it was inappropriate." Laura took a seat at the kitchen table and accepted the teacup Ted held out to her.

"Do you want to talk about inappropriate?" Jack stepped forward, and Alice kept a tight grip on his hand. "Going into a house where someone is currently robbing it. *That's* 'inappropriate.'"

"It's not inappropriate," Ted huffed. "It's dangerous. Foolish. Reckless."

"Ted," Laura said, but she didn't look up at him.

"It was, Laura. You could have gotten yourself killed."

"Don't be so dramatic." Laura sipped her tea and brushed an auburn curl from her forehead. "We just wanted to catch Mr. Hubbard in the act."

"Who?" Jack asked.

"Everyone in the book club has a different suspect in mind," Alice explained, "each with a different motive. Ruby thinks it's Mr. Hubbard, Ginny thinks it's Flo, and Ellie thinks it's a gang of criminals who retired here but decided to go back into business to supplement their pensions."

"This is like the AARP version of Clue," Jack muttered.

Ted laughed.

"It's not funny, Ted." Laura shot him a look.

Ted pointed at Jack. "He said it."

"Thanks, Dad."

"You did!"

"Boys, stop." Laura's teacup clinked against the saucer as she set it down. "Besides, the Orange Blossom Cove Bandit is Janet Ferguson."

"The senior supermodel?" Jack said.

Laura glared. "Supermodel? She's not *that* attractive."

Alice swatted his arm.

"Janet stopped by tonight," Ted said.

Laura's hazel eyes narrowed. "She *is* behind it."

"Mom," Jack said, "she was here when you guys were breaking into that house. So Janet can't be the bandit."

"Or maybe she came over to distract you while her accomplice was breaking into the Swansons'."

"She came over to join your book club, Mom. Listen to yourself. You sound…" Jack let his voice trail off as his mother's stare bore down on him.

"If you think my theory is so out in left field, who do *you* think is behind these thefts?"

"I don't know, Mom, but whoever took off across the backyard wasn't a typical seventy-year-old grandmother. They were moving super-fast."

"But they got a head start on you. You were sleeping."

"Unless they had a rocket-powered walker, there's no way they outran me."

Ted tried to cover his laughter with coughing.

Laura glared. "If you're not going to contribute constructively to the conversation, Mr. Stratton, please go into the living room."

Jack saw Alice's shoulders begin to shake, and he knew what that meant: she was about to start giggling. *Don't laugh or my mother will go through the roof,* he tried to communicate with his eyes.

"I'm sorry," Ted said. "I just pictured Flo trying to hold onto a rocket walker as it zoomed across the… Excuse me." He clamped his mouth closed and hurried out of the room.

"Well?" Laura's steady gaze landed on Jack. "Are you going to help me or not?"

"If I do, will you and the Golden Girl Commando Squad stand down?"

Alice pushed off from the counter and dashed toward the door. She was turning crimson, stifling a laugh. "I'm going…to check…on your dad." She disappeared.

Jack's mother folded her arms. "Agreed."

"Okay, then. I'll look into it."

Out in the living room, Ted roared with laughter.

Laura stood. "I'm going to go freshen up." She glowered at the living room door. "Please quiet down your father."

As his mother stomped down the hallway, Jack went into the living room. Both Alice and his father were red-faced and wiping away tears.

"Golden Girl Commando Squad." Ted giggled. "That's perfect."

"Knock it off, Dad. Mom's already upset." Jack turned to Alice. "And what about you?"

"I'm so sorry. I got the giggles and couldn't stop. *You* made me laugh."

Ted wiped his eyes. "It's your fault, Jack."

"It's not funny." Jack narrowed his eyes at Alice. "I still think you put my mom up to that stakeout."

"I had nothing to do with it, I swear." Alice's hands touched her chest. "I thought we were going to watch *Wheel of Fortune* or bake or something. Then all her friends came over dressed like ninja grannies."

Ted stamped his foot and laughed. "Stop! I can't hold back if you keep this up!"

The doorbell rang.

"Dad." Jack waggled his finger. "I'm serious. Quiet down or go outside."

Alice pressed her lips tightly together and looked at the floor. Her shoulders trembled.

With a sigh, Jack went to open the front door.

It was Gladys Crouse. She stepped inside without waiting for an invitation. "Is your mother back from the police station? How much was her bail?"

"She didn't get bailed out, Mrs. Crouse."

"They sent her straight to prison!" Gladys's face lit up as if she'd just gotten a gift.

Laura's bedroom door flew open. She marched down the hallway and stopped with one hand on her hip. "I didn't get bailed out because I did not get arrested—because I did *nothing* wrong."

"But I saw the four of you get taken away in the police car."

"The whole thing was a big misunderstanding, Mrs. Crouse." Ted stepped up next to his wife and slipped an arm around her waist.

"But you broke into the Swansons'. Why didn't you get arrested?"

"Because we didn't break into the Swansons'. We were looking for the real burglar."

"Well," Gladys grumbled, "what *I* heard is that you four missed the boat. There *was* a burglary at the Swansons'. Someone stole her sea turtle wind chime."

"I knew we saw a flashlight," Laura said. "Did you see anyone in the backyard?" she asked Alice.

"I was kind of busy running from the police."

Now it was Gladys's turn to put her hands on her hips. "Well, I guess you can chalk up another theft to the Orange Blossom Cove Bandit. I don't think your little book club is going to crack that riddle."

Laura stiffened. "We most certainly will. And now that my son has agreed to help, we'll know who's responsible very shortly."

Gladys peered up at Jack. "Are you a detective?"

"He's a policeman," Laura said proudly.

"I'm sure he's perfectly able to direct traffic, but solving crimes—"

Laura inhaled sharply. "He will solve it. Now, we were about to go to bed." She marched over and opened the front door.

Gladys turned to go, but stopped just outside. "Well, your son will have to find the bandit fast. How long is he here? A week? No offense, but how could he possibly catch the bandit when the entire police force hasn't found a clue?"

"Good night, Mrs. Crouse." Jack shut the door behind her.

Laura scrunched her shoulders and glared. "We'll show that busybody. I'll have Carl email his list to Alice. He's the one with the"—she swirled her hand above her head and whispered—"hairpiece. He's documented every item that's been stolen, and entered the whos, whats, and whens in a spreadsheet. And Jack, you should get on to bed now, so you can start first thing in the morning. I know you'll catch him."

"Talk about no pressure, Mom."

"Don't be silly." Laura squeezed his hand. "I know you can do it."

The look on her face made Jack's chest tighten. If there was one person on the planet he most didn't want to disappoint, it was his mom. But how was he going to catch this bandit in less than a week?

17

THEORIES AND LISTS

Jack woke up to the smell of eggs and the sound of pans rattling. He rolled out of bed, went to the bathroom, and then walked, bleary-eyed, into the kitchen.

He hadn't expected company, but there they were. Ellie, Carl, Ginny, Ruby, Alice, and his father were all crammed around the kitchen table while his mother stood at the stove.

"Clear him a space," said Ruby.

"You can sit right here, Jackie." Ellie pointed to the only open seat.

Jack rubbed his eyes and scowled at Alice and his father, who looked as if they were about to suffer another laughing fit.

As Jack sat down, his mother plopped a heaping plate of food in front of him, along with a large cup of coffee and a glass of orange juice. Jack closed his eyes and said a quick prayer.

When he looked up, all eyes were on him. His mother laid some papers beside his plate.

"Carl printed out the master list," she explained.

"He's recorded everything." Ellie patted the back of Carl's hand. "He's very detail-oriented."

"He emailed me a copy, too," Alice said.

"It's all there," Carl said. "But I still say we were close to figuring out the pattern." He tapped the papers. "Another stakeout and—"

Jack held up his left hand and picked up his coffee with his right. "No more stakeouts. None. Period." To make sure he got his point across, he made eye contact with everyone in the room, particularly his mother. Then he took a sip of coffee. "What do you mean, pattern?"

"Carl thinks there's a pattern to the thefts." Ginny fiddled with her glasses cord.

"There is," Carl said confidently.

"So we have stakeouts to try to catch the thieves," Ellie added.

Everyone started talking at once about who they thought was responsible.

"Wait a second." Jack waved a forkful of eggs. "I don't want to get this information by committee."

Ruby leaned in. "But we each have a theory."

Jack sighed. It was clear he wasn't going anywhere until he'd heard them out. "Carl," he said, "you wrote all this up. Why don't you start?"

Ellie squeezed Carl's hand, and he puffed his chest out like Patton about to address the troops.

"Well, that's a detailed list of everything that's been stolen. It has dates, whose house it was stolen from, and what was taken. Now, I'm sure that some people who put things on that list are flat-out lying—"

"Carl." Ginny clapped her hands together like a librarian calling for quiet. "They could be mistaken. We have no proof—"

"Oh, come on," Carl grumbled. "Who would have stolen that figurine from Janet?"

"I gave her that cat figurine." Ginny put her hand on her chest. "It was a lovely hardened faux-hair over antique plaster of Paris."

Ted and Alice had moved to the sink. Ted whispered something to Alice, and she clamped her hand over her mouth.

"I agree with Carl." Laura cast a quick behave-yourself glance at her husband. "I don't trust her."

"Okay, so my mom and Carl think that Janet is behind the thefts."

"I don't." Carl leaned on the table. "I just said she's lying about the missing figurine."

Ellie raised her hand.

"Yes?" Jack asked.

"Can I say my theory?"

Everyone started talking again.

Ted held up his hands. He was in full-on teacher mode and quickly quieted the crowd. "This is how we're going to proceed. Jack has the list of thefts and each of your theories. He and I are going to go over this list today, and we can all meet up again tomorrow for a follow-up."

Everyone started protesting, but Ted's stern gaze was enough to quiet everyone except Ruby.

"What makes you Watson to his Holmes?" Ruby asked, her right eyebrow arched.

Jack had to hide his smile as he waited for his father's reply.

Ted squared his shoulders. It appeared he liked the analogy. "We've done it before. As a matter of fact, this case is actually a step down for us. Jack and I solved the Stacy Shaw disappearance. You can Google it."

"And Jack just caught the Giant Killer," Alice said proudly.

"Alice is being modest," Jack said. "She has her own—"

Alice shook her head, and Jack stopped talking.

"Do you expect the rest of us to just sit on our hands?" Carl groused.

"For right now, I think we should follow Ted's plan," Laura said. "Let's vote. All in favor?"

Ellie's hand shot up immediately. Ginny's hand went up next, and Ruby's soon followed.

Ellie nudged Carl, and finally he raised his hand too.

"Wonderful. We'll meet back here tomorrow," Ted said.

Laura saw everyone out while Jack finished his breakfast.

Once they were all gone, Jack raised an eyebrow at his father. "What did you say to Alice at the sink?"

Ted chuckled. "You should have seen that cat figurine that Ginny gave Janet. It's got fake hair that makes it look like you took a dead cat and dipped it in shellac. It even has red eyes. It's like a possessed old-fashioned doll—super-creepy."

Jack laughed. "Well, thanks for clearing the room. You know, trying to figure out who did this is going to take a lot longer than a day—if I can do it at all. Do you think there's any chance these guys will just let it go? I mean, have you looked at Carl's list? Almost everything stolen was worth less than fifty bucks."

Ted shook his head. "They wouldn't care if it was a quarter. To them, it's the principle of the thing. They want to know who it is."

Jack sighed. "What if I don't figure it out? How's Mom going to take it?"

Ted whistled low. "I'll deal with your mother. She'll…" He trailed off, and a reassuring smile appeared on his face. "She'll be fine. Fine."

"You really do need some acting lessons, Dad." Jack put his plate in the dishwasher. "I guess I *have* to solve this mystery. I'd rather get kicked in the head than disappoint Mom. Well, we'd better get to it. You know Alice is coming with us, right?"

Alice's face lit up.

"I'd love to have her help," Ted said.

"Hey," Jack said to Alice, "why didn't you want me to tell them that you have your own private investigation business? And we *both* caught the Giant Killer."

Alice shrugged. "Because your mom's so proud of you. These are her friends and you're her baby. This means a lot to her. Besides, I didn't want to take any limelight from her golden boy in action." Alice stood with her hands on her hips and laughed.

Jack looked at those dimples that made him melt every time and smiled.

Ted wrapped an arm around Alice's shoulders and gave her a big hug. "Thank you for thinking of my wife." He winked at Jack. "There are plenty of fish in the sea, my boy, but this one's a keeper."

Alice lifted herself up on her toes. She was beaming.

Jack knew that for a young woman who had spent much of her childhood in foster care and had lost her own father, those were the sweetest words his dad ever could have said.

18

SPECIAL DELIVERY

Dixon slowed to a crawl and waited until he saw the green rental car pull out of the driveway. Ted Stratton was driving, and a young woman was sitting in the back. The man who chased him the night before was in the passenger seat. He craned his neck and tried to see into the backseat. He wasn't certain, but he thought he saw the dog next to the young woman. It didn't matter. Even if they left the mutt behind, he could deal with a dog.

Dixon smiled. Auntie had said just the four of them were there. *Now that they're gone, Laura Stratton is home alone.*

He parked along the curb. A few old men were out walking little dogs. He eyed them with disdain. They were like seagulls, pot-bellied with skinny legs, hoping for any little thing to break the monotony of the end of their days.

It was only nine fifteen, but the morning was already sweltering; even with the car windows open, the temperature in the car climbed quickly. Dixon cursed the broken air conditioner. He hated this old car. But the payment from this package would be enough for a down payment on a new truck. All he had to do was get the statue.

He winced as he pulled the baseball hat lower to cover his eyes. It tugged on the bandages, and the pain fueled his anger. He grabbed the cardboard box off the seat, got out of the car, and shut the door. When he saw his reflection in the driver's side mirror, he frowned. His all-brown getup looked like the uniform of a delivery driver, but his Egyptian tattoo stood out on his neck. *I should've slapped some of Auntie's makeup on that.* He turned sideways to check his back. His pants bulged only slightly over the gun tucked into his waistband.

An old lady on the sidewalk across from him stopped and looked his way. Dixon tipped his head down and headed up the walkway to Laura Stratton's house. His heart was beating hard in anticipation. He had killed other people, of course—starting with his grandfather. And he had to admit that he liked watching them die. But this time was different—better. His eyes narrowed, his brow creased, and his scalp hurt. He was going to kill the old crow who'd hurt him, and he was going to really enjoy it. He couldn't care less what Auntie said. He'd *try* to make it look like an accident—but it would be a very *painful* accident.

He rapped on the door absentmindedly, lost in thought, picturing the ways he could kill her. *Maybe she could fall and smash her little head? Or...they have a car. Maybe it slipped into neutral and pinned her to the wall? Slowly crushing the life out of her...*

"Can I help you?"

Dixon jumped. Laura Stratton stood in the doorway, smiling. He hadn't even heard the door open. He stood there, blinking. Did she recognize him? She didn't look scared.

"Are you delivering that?" She pointed at the box in his hand.

"Yes." He cleared his throat. "I have a package for you."

From his pocket, he pulled out a phone message pad he'd found in a drawer at his aunt's house. He was careful not to let Laura see the front while he pretended to search his pockets for a pen. Finally, he looked at her and did his best to appear flustered. "I need you to sign. Do you have a pen?"

"Certainly. One second."

Laura walked into the house, and Dixon slipped through the door behind her.

The screen door clicked closed, and Laura glanced over her shoulder. She gave a little start when she saw him inside the foyer.

"Do you mind waiting there?" Her eyes tightened, and she looked nervous.

Dixon grinned. "Not at all. I'll wait right here."

Laura seemed to relax. "Thank you."

"But I'm letting all your cold air out." Dixon reached back and shut the door. "I don't live in a barn, right?" His grandfather had screamed those words in his face right before Dixon punched him in the throat.

Dixon smiled.

Laura swallowed and took a step back. "Let me check if my husband has a pen. He's in the kitchen."

Lie. Lie. Lie.

Dixon's smile grew.

You're still going to die, die, die.

A clicking sounded on the tiles down the hallway. *Maybe Laura isn't alone after all? But who else could be here?*

The clicking grew louder, and then the biggest dog Curtis Dixon had ever seen in his life came into view. It looked as if someone had pumped a German Shepherd full of the same secret formula that had made Captain America. The dog's back was broad and muscular, and on its chest was a patch of golden brown in the shape of a shield.

A low rumble began deep in the dog's chest, and its muzzle twisted into a snarl, revealing teeth that looked as large as a tiger's.

"It's okay, Lady." Laura reached out to calm the dog, but it still took a step toward Dixon.

Dixon reached back and opened the door.

The dog took another step forward and sniffed. Its eyes narrowed, and Dixon knew the beast had caught his scent the night before.

He turned and bolted.

Claws scratched on the tiles behind him.

Laura was shouting something, but he didn't hear. He was focused on his car. He heard the screen door click shut, but his relief at that sound was short-lived. A second later, the door was ripped off its hinges as the beast jumped through it. Dixon didn't look back, but he heard the door crash to the walkway.

He sprinted to the car and dove through the passenger window. Jaws snapped at the air behind him. Pain shot through his head as it bashed into the driver's side door.

The beast put its front paws on the car door and roared. Dixon fumbled for the gun stuck in the back of his pants.

Huffing and puffing, Laura raced over and seized the dog's collar. "Lady! Lady!"

The dog got off the car, but kept barking. It pressed against Laura's legs and looked as if it was actually trying to move her away from the car.

Dixon grabbed the gun and was about to yank it out when he heard a man's voice. "Laura? Are you okay?"

It was an old coot with a poodle, calling to her from across the street. The poodle was barking too.

"I'm fine. Everything's fine, Bernie." Laura peered into the car. "I'm so sorry. Are you okay? She's never acted like this before."

Dixon scowled. More old people were staring. Across the street, a couple had opened their front door and shuffled out.

"I'm all right. The dog just... Forget about it." Dixon yanked out his keys and started the car.

Laura made a face. "I hate to ask, but...can I have my package?"

Dixon didn't know what to do. The package was fake. Should he just drive off? All the old ghouls were staring at him, but if he left it with her...

"I'm sorry. I made a mistake." He pointed to the label. "It's 11 Banyan Bay. This is Banyan Breeze Drive. I just noticed the street sign."

Laura Stratton gave him a look of pity, as though he were the sorriest creature on the planet. "Oh, after all that. I'm so sorry. Are you sure you're okay?"

Dixon started the car and tried not to scowl. Right now, his every instinct told him to draw his gun and shoot her, the stupid dog, and every old bag on the block; he had to channel all his remaining energy into resisting those instincts. "I'm fine." He forced a smile.

But as he drove away, his smile changed. Like Pinocchio, the wooden grin turned real when he thought: *But I'm coming back. And when I do, you sure as hell won't be fine.*

19

THE SHADOW MAN

Ted parked the car in Mrs. Manning's driveway. "Well, here we are. Why did you want to come here first?"

Jack tapped the papers in his hand. "I've split the thefts on this sheet into two groups. The lesser group involves items taken from outside the home—and almost everything on the list falls into that category. There are only three cases where the thief actually went into the house. There's a huge difference between the two types of crime."

"Petty theft versus breaking and entering?" Alice said.

"Exactly. So I want to start with the serious crimes first—and that includes Betty Manning. It says a necklace was stolen from the bedroom, and that Mrs. Manning saw the thief, though Carl didn't list a physical description. Do you know Mrs. Manning, Dad?"

"Everyone in Orange Blossom knows everyone else. They have some event going on every day at the community center. Sometimes twice a day."

"I thought you were supposed to *relax* in retirement. What's she like?"

"She's one of the good ones. Nice. Chatty."

Jack and Alice followed Ted to the door. Ted rang the doorbell.

"Do you mind making the introductions?" Jack asked him.

"Sure."

The door opened, and a shapely young woman dressed in hospital scrubs appeared in the entranceway. Her name tag, which read "Kiara Gonzalez," stood out on her ample chest.

She stepped closer to Jack and smiled broadly. "May I help you?" Her brown eyes sparkled.

"I, ah…" Jack was taken off guard.

Ted waved. "Good morning. Is Betty in?"

Kiara nodded. "May I have your names, please?"

"Ted and Jack Stratton. And Alice Campbell."

"One moment." Kiara kept the door open as she disappeared into a room on the right.

Alice shot Jack a sideways scowl and let her mouth hang open, imitating him. "I, ah…"

"What? I thought it was going to be a little old grandmother opening the door. It threw me."

Ted coughed to cover his grin.

A couple of seconds later, Kiara reappeared. "Mrs. Manning will see you now."

They walked into the living room. Mrs. Manning smiled as they entered. The tiny, round-faced senior was hooked up to a dialysis machine.

Jack and Alice stopped short. Ted kept going. "Good morning, Betty. This is my son, Jack, and his girlfriend, Alice."

Betty smiled at Jack. "I've heard nice things about you."

"Thank you, ma'am. If now isn't a good time, we can come back."

"I never know how I'm going to feel. Now's fine." She gestured to a chair, and Ted sat next to her.

The sunny living room was a mix of bright colors and flower patterns. Accent pillows that looked to be handmade sat on every couch and chair, and photos of smiling grandchildren filled the shelves and dotted the tables and walls as well.

Kiara slipped off down the hallway, and Jack and Alice sat opposite Ted on a loveseat.

"What brings you by?" Betty asked.

"Actually," Jack said, "my mother asked us to look into some missing property."

"For the book club? Oh, they've been by several times. I agree with Ellie—I think all these thefts are the work of a gang." Betty's hand went to her throat. "Did you find my necklace?"

"Not yet, ma'am. But you said that someone broke in and stole it. I just had a couple of questions about that night."

"It's been a couple of months past now. The necklace isn't worth much, monetarily, but to me…" She seemed to get a little frailer as she crossed her feet and folded her hands in her lap. "To me it's priceless, and I'd love to get it back."

"Where exactly was this necklace when it was stolen?" Jack asked.

"In my jewelry case in my bedroom. That's a big clue for you."

"What is?" Alice leaned forward.

"Whoever the thief is, they're not too familiar with jewelry. I would think they would try to study up and get to know what things are worth. In order to…oh, what's that word? Pawn it. You'd think they'd be knowledgeable, but this one wasn't."

"What makes you say that?" Jack asked.

"Because they left the rest of my jewelry alone. Much more valuable stuff, too. The necklace they stole was a present from my father when I was little. He worked at a shoe factory. Can you believe that we used to have those? Here? In America? But he did. It was for my thirteenth birthday. It was a simple silver chain with an oval red hyacinth."

"A hyacinth flower?" Jack asked.

"A hyacinth is also a zircon," Betty explained. "It wasn't an expensive gemstone, but it looked like it was. That's the clue. I'm sure of it. When you looked in my jewelry box, that necklace just glowed like one of the queen's jewels."

"Can you tell me about that night?" Jack asked.

"It was last…" Betty looked down at her hands and closed her eyes. "It was close to my birthday, so that would have been just around Thanksgiving. The day of the theft, I hadn't been able to take my usual nap because of all the racket, so I went to bed early. I was sound asleep when I was awakened by a faint sound in the kitchen. It sounded like the wind. I thought I must have left a window open, so I got out of bed to go and close it. I was surprised to find all the windows closed. I checked them one by one. I nearly keeled over when I looked out in the yard and saw a man. That is not normal in these parts at that time of night."

"What did he look like?" Ted asked. "Was he big? Was he out near the pond?"

Jack cleared his throat and shot his father a look that he hoped would get him to stop talking. His father was handing Betty details, and Jack wanted her unfiltered recollection.

Betty nodded. "He was the same height as Neil, my late husband. Same build, too. When Neil was younger of course." She smiled at the memory. "Neil's long passed, but I'm certain. This man alongside the pond—it looked as if he was walking along the path toward the Jacksons'."

"Did you recognize him or notice anything particular about him?"

Betty shook her head. "My eyes aren't what they used to be, and it was dark. He was a shadow."

"You mentioned you couldn't nap earlier that day. Why not?"

"They were putting in those bushes." Betty pointed to the small bushes outside her window. "They were here all day digging and making a big production out of it."

Kiara walked in with a bamboo tray of iced tea, water, and assorted cookies. As she set it down on the coffee table, she leaned so close to Jack that her breath tickled the skin on his neck. "May I please have a moment with you?" she whispered.

Alice stiffened beside him.

Jack nodded. "Please excuse me."

Kiara walked out into the hallway, and Jack followed her. He pulled up short when she suddenly stopped and turned around. She stood so close to him that she was practically speaking into his mouth.

"I need to talk with you," she whispered, "but you must promise me something." She grabbed his forearm and stepped even closer, if that was possible.

The personal space that Jack preferred was shattered. He didn't think she realized the awkwardness, but Kiara pressed against him. Her perfume rose to his nose.

"It's about the necklace." Her brown eyes rounded.

Jack angled his head slightly, and once again she was whispering in his ear.

"When Mrs. Manning told me about the break-in and the missing necklace, I got worried for her safety. Her daughter asked me to call her about anything of concern, so I did."

"Are you her full-time nurse?"

"I am. Mrs. Manning is getting frail, so I worry about her. Especially at night when she's alone. She can't afford round-the-clock care."

"What did her daughter say?"

"She doesn't remember her mother ever having a necklace like that." Kiara cast a nervous look back at Mrs. Manning. "Her daughter comes here every other weekend to visit. She thinks maybe her mom is just mistaken."

"So her daughter doesn't think a necklace was even stolen?"

Kiara sighed; her breath tickled Jack's ear. "She thinks her mother imagined it in a vivid dream or got confused. Please don't say anything. Mrs. Manning is a little worried about forgetting things. She gets agitated when anyone brings it up."

"I won't say a word."

As Jack walked back into the living room, Betty was patting the back of Ted's hand. "Thank you so much for stopping by."

Ted set his drink down. "All set?" he asked Jack as he got to his feet.

Jack nodded. "It was nice to meet you, ma'am."

"Please let me know if you find my necklace."

"I'll do my best, ma'am."

Betty gave Ted a smile with her lips pressed tightly together, and Kiara led them out.

When they got to the car, Alice said, "So, Jack. What did the nurse say when she was trying to climb on top of you?"

Ted chuckled.

"She didn't want Mrs. Manning to hear and get upset."

"Well, I'm sure *you* heard her, seeing as the words only had to travel, what, a millimeter from her mouth to yours? For a second, I thought she was giving you mouth-to-mouth resuscitation."

Jack smiled at Alice and ran through his conversation with Kiara. "It's the reason I wanted to talk with Mrs. Manning first. The stolen necklace doesn't fit the pattern of the other crimes. I think Kiara is right: Mrs. Manning just got confused."

"But what about the man she saw at the pond?" Alice asked.

"I think she may have been confused about the shadow man too."

"Well, I'm glad you didn't say anything to Betty," Ted said. "With the dialysis, the last thing she needs to worry about is if her mind is going."

"Ready for the next one?" Alice said.

"Wagons ho!" Ted laughed and pointed forward. His hand trembled slightly as he held it out.

"You feeling okay, Dad?"

"Me? Fit as a fiddle." Ted looked straight ahead. "One anomaly down, two to go."

20

GIVE THE MAN A CIGAR

"Six Cypress." Jack looked out the window at the little ranch house. "You sure there isn't a different house we can go to?" Ted asked. "What's wrong with this one?" Alice asked.

"Brad Cox," Ted muttered. "The man just rubs me the wrong way."

"Well, besides Mrs. Ferguson and Betty, he's the only other person who had something stolen from *inside* his house. And he said he saw someone."

Alice looked at the sheet. "He was interviewed by the police too. He listed one thousand dollars in cash and two watches as stolen."

Ted sighed. "You're in charge."

"Thanks, Dad."

Brad Cox came to the door in a pair of Hawaiian shorts and no shirt. He was a short man with a beach ball belly. His skin was darkly tanned and leathery. The scent of coconut tanning lotion filled the air.

"Good to see you, Ted. What can I do for you?" He leaned against the doorframe.

"Actually," Jack stuck his hand out, "I wanted to speak with you, sir. My name's Jack Stratton. This is my girlfriend, Alice."

Brad shook Jack's hand and then looked back and forth between Jack and his father. "He your nephew or something?" he asked Ted.

"Jack's my son."

Brad raised an eyebrow. "Good thing he didn't get your height." He laughed at his own dig.

Jack could already understand why his father hadn't wanted to see Brad Cox. In less than ten seconds, he already disliked the man.

"What did you want to ask me?"

"It's about the break-in you had after Christmas."

"Are you a cop?" Brad's wrinkles deepened.

"No. I'm—"

"Don't tell me you're helping those Miss Marple wannabes." Brad chuckled. "Are you two the Hardy Boys? Then she must be Nancy Drew." He laughed so hard he started hacking and coughing.

"You saw the thief?" Jack asked.

Brad pounded his chest and coughed again. "Come on, guys. I'm kidding. Lighten up."

"Did you see the thief?" Jack repeated.

"Just a glimpse of his back. He was hightailing it around the bushes. He was a little guy. Had jeans, a green shirt, black hair. You know what that means?"

Jack shook his head.

"The green shirts here ain't got green cards, if you know what I mean."

"He's talking about the lawn maintenance crew," Ted said. "They wear green uniforms."

"Lawn maintenance?" Brad scoffed. "Fancy name for grass monkeys."

Jack's anger flared, but his father reacted before he did.

"Those men work harder than you ever did, Brad."

Brad put his hands up and stepped back. "It was a joke."

Jack stepped in front of his father. "Are you sure that's what you saw?"

"Ted, I was kidding. Don't go getting all politically correct on me." Brad put his hands down. "I saw what I said I saw. Small guy with a green shirt. He stole a thousand dollars and two of my watches from my nightstand." He turned back to Ted. "Are you upset I thought he was your nephew?"

"No." Ted adjusted his glasses. "Your language was offensive."

"Look." Brad hiked up his shorts. "I don't mean nothing by it. They do a good job when they're working. And look at your kid. He's like a foot taller than you."

"Do you normally keep a thousand dollars in cash in the house?" Jack asked.

"No. I was getting my bathroom redone. I even got an estimate. Insurance company still hasn't paid my claim."

"Thank you for your time."

"That's it?" Brad said.

"Yes. Thank you," Jack repeated. He walked back toward the car, and his father and Alice followed.

"I hope you get my stuff back," Brad called out. "And I didn't mean nothing about you two looking so different. But you know what they say—Momma's baby, Daddy's maybe." He let out a bawdy guffaw, which was cut off when Alice and Ted spun around.

Brad ducked back inside and slammed the door.

Ted marched back toward the door, with Alice right beside him.

Jack grabbed his arm. "Dad, come on. Alice, you too."

They both glared at the house.

"You were right," Jack said. "He's an ass. But what are you going to do? Punch him in the nose?"

"If you hadn't had the alligator taken away, I would have brought Brad down to the pond," Ted grumbled.

Jack laughed. "Now I see where I get my anger issues from."

"Don't be silly. You got those from your mother."

Jack laughed harder.

"What a disgusting racist," Ted said as they got back in the car.

"And a rude scumbag," Alice added.

"You can include insurance fraud on Brad's list of faults," Jack said.

Alice leaned forward. "What?"

"I'm sure the insurance company thinks so too," Jack said. "That's why they haven't paid his claim."

"How can you be sure?" Ted asked.

"The cash for a home repair job and the amount of money. Most places don't want cash anymore. And most people want to pay with credit cards or with a check so they have a record of payment if there's a problem."

"I didn't think home insurance covered cash."

"It can, but there's a limit. Want to guess what it is?"

"A thousand dollars?"

"Give the man a cigar. Either way, I think Brad's credibility is zero."

21

A SINGING FROG

As Ted drove away from Brad's, Alice sat forward. "You know, I just can't get over the work Carl put into this list. Everything's categorized and color-coded."

"If every crime got as much attention when I was a cop, my arrest rate would've skyrocketed," Jack said. "What did Carl do before he retired?"

Ted chuckled. "Accountant. But it's not just him. The whole book club is into it. Your mother made the first version of that spreadsheet, except she did it the old-fashioned way—on a bunch of index cards. Carl and Ellie put it together in Excel."

"Mrs. Stratton did a great job," Alice said.

"She's a mystery nut," Ted said proudly. "She and Jack used to watch them together all the time. So when someone stole Beverly Nash's solar rooster a year ago and all hell broke loose, your mother picked up her deerstalker."

"Her what?" Alice asked.

"Deerstalker." Ted chuckled. "That's what they call the hat Sherlock Holmes wears."

"Wait a second," Jack said. "Did you say someone stole a solar rooster?"

"Yup. Truth be told, most everyone was glad someone shut the thing up."

"What's a solar rooster?" Alice asked.

Ted shook his head and sighed. "It was this awful solar-powered whirligig thing that crowed when the sun came up. Every morning that thing went off and got the whole neighborhood out of bed. But Beverly loved it—even offered a reward for its return. And your mother's book club looked into it like the Lindbergh kidnapping, Hoffa's disappearance, and who shot JFK all rolled into one."

"For a rooster?" Jack said.

"You'll understand when you get older."

"You've been saying that my whole life. When will I understand?"

"When will he be older?" Alice joked.

Jack rolled his eyes. They were ganging up on him.

"So, where am I supposed to be driving next, anyway?" Ted asked.

Alice fingered the list. "The only other person who had something stolen from inside the house was Janet Ferguson."

"Ah, yes," said Ted. "The infamous Frankenstein's monster cat figurine. But what about Tom Cummings? He had a post-hole digger taken from his garage."

"The post-hole digger didn't require a break-in," Jack said. "Carl noted that Tom Cummings left his garage door open, so I'm classifying that one with the outdoor petty thefts. For now anyway."

"Fair enough," Ted said. "But if we're going to visit Janet Ferguson, perhaps you'd better speak to your mother first. Laura and Janet get along like gasoline and a match."

Jack's mouth twisted into a wide grin. "Actually, we don't need to see Janet again just yet. I have an idea, but I'll need to pick up a couple of things to make it work. Do you have a pet store around here?"

***

Ted parked in front of the pet store. "Can I see the list again?" As he reached for the list, his hand trembled.

"Why don't you both wait here in the car?" Jack shot Alice a glance. "I'll be right out."

Alice nodded and leaned over the seat to look at the list with Jack's father.

Jack went into the pet store and grabbed what he needed. By the time he came back out, he'd settled on the rest of the plan.

"That was fast," Alice said.

"Are you all set?" Ted asked.

Jack held up his bag. "One extra-strong dog leash, and one dog collar with a built-in locator in case the leash isn't as strong as advertised."

"Smart man." Ted smiled.

"I'm so sorry. Again," Alice added.

"It's not your fault that Lady's as strong as a horse."

As Jack buckled in, Ted asked, "Where to next, Detective?"

"I need to find a place that sells statues. Is there a hardware store around here? Somewhere with a lawn and garden section. We can head home after that, if you're getting tired of all this."

"Who, me? I'm having the time of my life. Besides, figuring this out means a lot to your mother."

"I get that, Dad. Believe me, I get it."

A few minutes later, they were walking down the wide, long aisles of the lawn and garden section of a Home Mart. They passed shelves of garden gnomes, birdbaths, and wind chimes.

Jack stopped in front of a large garden gnome feeding a larger-than-life-sized duck.

"We only have a small backyard," Ted said.

"Mom's got a birthday coming up..." Jack grinned. "The perfect gift, I think."

"Jack, if you buy her that monstrosity, I swear I'm giving Alice two season passes to the Darrington ballet."

Alice giggled, and Jack laughed.

"You win."

Jack moved on. His eyes lit up when he saw a frog statue with a sign that read:

ADD MUSIC TO YOUR GARDEN
WITH A SINGING FROG.
SURPRISE YOUR GUESTS
AND WARN OFF PESTS!
SINGING FROG WITH BUILT-IN MOTION SENSOR
ON SALE $39.99

Jack picked up the display model. The statue was twenty inches tall, a foot wide, and hollow; Jack's hand fit easily inside the bottom. He turned it on and waved his hand in front of its mouth. The frog loudly croaked "At the Hop" by Danny & the Juniors.

Ted made a face. "I hope you're kidding, because I wasn't."

"Nope." Jack grinned and picked up a brightly colored lawn pinwheel, too. He blew on it. A rainbow of color sparkled as it spun. "Perfect."

22

WHAT HAPPENED TO THE DOOR?

Jack held the door open for Alice as they followed his father into the house.

"Laura?" Ted shouted. "What happened to the screen door?"

Jack's mother was in the living room, speaking softly to Lady and holding on to her collar. "I put it in the garage."

"You lugged that thing to the garage all by yourself?"

"I couldn't just leave it on the walkway."

Ted looked confused. "But why is the door not on the house?"

Jack and Alice both looked down at Lady and sighed. "Lady."

Lady lowered her head and whimpered.

"It's not her fault." Laura rubbed Lady's neck, and the giant dog looked up at her with intense brown eyes, her long tongue hanging out of her mouth. "The delivery man needed a pen and followed me inside. Lady barked and ran at him. I'm sure she was just trying to protect me."

"Is the delivery man okay?" Ted ran a hand over his mouth.

"He's fine. Just shaken up. The door, on the other hand…"

"I'll pay for the door, Mom. Sorry, Dad."

"I'm just glad everyone's okay," Ted said.

Laura walked over to Ted, kissed his cheek, and whispered something in his ear. He leaned over and whispered back, and Laura wrinkled her brow in concern.

She touched Ted's cheek with the back of her hand. "Do you want something to eat?"

Ted shook his head. "I'm fine. I'll let Jack fill you in about his plan." He excused himself, headed to his bedroom, and shut the door.

Jack turned to follow his father, but his mother gently tapped his shoulder. "He's going to take a quick nap," she whispered. "He doesn't like to broadcast it."

"I'm so sorry about Lady, Mrs. Stratton," Alice said. "I don't know what could have gotten into her. She's usually so well-behaved."

Jack stifled a laugh. "I'm just glad she didn't eat the guy."

Lady trotted over to the mantel, gazed up at it, and whined.

"Don't you get started on that again. It's just a statue." Jack moved the gecko statue, and Lady barked.

Alice patted Lady and spoke as if she were talking to a frightened child. "It's okay. It's not real."

"It's a symbol of my winning streak," Laura said. "The casino in the Bahamas presented it to us. I don't normally gamble, but we won the cruise and it included games at the casino." She stood up a little straighter. "I couldn't believe I won that trip. I never—"

Lady rose up on her haunches and put her paws on the mantel, pushing the lime-green lizard sideways. It tumbled off the mantel, and Jack barely caught it by one of its legs before it hit the floor.

"Lady." Jack groaned. He carefully placed the little lizard back in its place.

Alice grabbed Lady's collar. "I'm so, so sorry."

"No worries," Laura said, though her drawn face didn't match her words. "Good reflexes, Jack. Lady and I will just have to disagree about that little statue. For me, it's kind of a symbol of my unexpected good fortune. It's too bad the yellow in its back doesn't match anything in the room."

Jack turned the statute toward the front door so more of the lime-green showed and less lemon.

"I guess Lady still hasn't gotten over her fear of geckos," Alice said.

"Maybe I should put the statue in the den while you're here," Laura suggested.

Jack motioned to Alice. "Why don't we leave it where it is and put Lady in her room for a little while?"

Lady whined as Alice led her into the bedroom.

Laura waited until Alice closed the door behind her. Then she spoke to Jack in a low voice. "I want Alice to feel at home, Jack, and if Lady has to stay in the bedroom, how will that make her feel? Besides, it's not the dog's fault. She's just getting acclimated. It's a lot of change for her, and I'm sure that plane ride was unsettling."

"Whatever you do," Jack said, "don't bring up that plane ride around Lady."

The doorbell rang, and Laura went to answer it. It was Ruby and Ginny from the book club. They were flushed and out of breath. "Hi, Laura. Where's Alice?"

"In the bedroom. What's going on?"

Alice stepped back out into the hallway. "Is everything okay?"

"No time to explain," Ruby said. "We need Alice to do us that favor we talked about—right now. Ellie and Carl are on their way. They'll fill you in." She turned to Alice. "Can you help us, honey?"

"What do you need?"

"Come on. We'll talk on the way." Ruby took her by the hand and led her out the door. Ginny followed.

"Alice? Are you okay with this?" Jack called after her.

Alice's green eyes were wide, but she gave him a little wave and a thumbs-up.

After Laura had shut the door, Jack raised an eyebrow at her. "What exactly was that all about? If this is another stakeout..."

"Oh, Jack, I'm sure it's nothing like that. I guess Ellie will explain when she gets here."

"You really don't know? Ruby said it was a favor you talked about. What could Alice help with?"

"Maybe a computer problem? I'm going to put some tea on for Carl and Ellie. I'm sure they'll clear everything up."

Jack knew he shouldn't worry—after all, Alice was heading out with two of his mother's friends. But as he looked at the front door, his stomach tightened.

23

TAKEN TO THE CLEANERS

"Laura's positive it's her," Ruby said. They looked out the windows of the car at the largest house in the community.

"Her? Her who? The lady who lives there?" Alice pointed at the huge home. "I don't think she needs to steal *anything*."

"Money is not Janet's motive." Ginny frowned. "I don't like speaking ill of people, but that woman has an ax to grind with everyone in the community. We all try to include her in things, but she finds faults in everyone and everything. I keep trying to befriend her, but she has no interest in building trust."

"Is that why you gave her that cat figurine?" Ruby reached over and squeezed her friend's hand. "Bless your heart, Ginny."

"What happened, Ruby?" Alice leaned forward from the backseat.

"Ginny had a spring tea. It was lovely. Everything was beautifully done. Beautifully."

"Thank you, Ruby."

"It was! The finger sandwiches, the tea, the tablescapes—perfect. We all wore floral dresses and hats. She invited everyone, even Janet. We had an afternoon like proper ladies of London. But for all of Ginny's trouble, Janet had the gall to report that Ginny's roses were over the limit!"

"There's a limit on roses?"

"Not on the number of roses, but on their height. Ginny's rosebushes were too tall. She had to cut them way back and lost all their beautiful blooms. Those bushes may never recover. You wouldn't know this, but it is very difficult to grow any kind of rose in Florida."

"How do you know Janet reported her?"

"Gladys told us," Ginny said.

Alice rocked her head from side to side. "I don't know if I'd believe Gladys."

"Why not?"

"She's the busybody always stirring up trouble, right? And she knows Mrs. Stratton doesn't get along with Mrs. Ferguson, so it makes sense she'd blame Mrs. Ferguson, doesn't it? Just saying."

"Well…I normally don't listen to Gladys, but in this case I do think she was telling the truth. This is a gated community, and Ginny's roses beautified it. When they bloomed, the walkers would be sure to plan their route so they could pass by. Folks would bring visitors over to see them. They were an attraction, for goodness' sake!

Who else but sourball Janet would take something away from all of us like that? We finally have the time to stop and smell the roses, and she took them!" Ruby huffed.

"That's terrible about the roses, but I'm sorry, I'm not going to help you guys with your rose vendetta," Alice said firmly. "Let's go back to the Strattons' house."

"This isn't about the roses. Janet lied about the cat figurine. She said it was stolen, but it wasn't. We need your help to prove it."

"How do you know she lied?"

Ruby raised one eyebrow. "From the look on Janet's face when she told us about the theft. Everyone in the book club was canvassing the neighborhood, looking for anyone who could have had something stolen. We asked Janet if she was missing anything. She said no, but just as she was about to shut the door, she acted like she was hit from a bolt out of the blue. She practically screamed, 'The cat! The cat has been stolen!'"

"I thought it was more like a kitten—just adorable," Ginny said.

"It was." Ruby placed a comforting hand on her shoulder, but as Ginny looked down, Ruby looked back at Alice, made a face, and shook her head.

"I still don't understand why we're here," Alice said.

"Laura's always wanted to get a look around for that cat," Ruby explained. "She thinks Janet still has it. If we find it, we can prove she faked its theft!"

Ruby and Ginny got out of the car and started toward the house, and Alice reluctantly followed. "Wait…I thought you were going to let Jack and his father look into this."

"We are, but this is too good to pass up."

Ginny clapped her hands together. "You're going undercover."

Alice practically tripped over her feet, but Ruby grabbed her elbow and pulled her upright.

"I'm what?"

"Going undercover," Ginny repeated. "We ran into Janet at the community center, and she said she had to fire her cleaning service."

"I saw the opportunity, and you know what they say…" Ruby smiled like Tony Robbins. "Carpe diem!"

Alice shook her head. "This is a bad idea."

"It's brilliant." Ruby put her hands on her hips. "Besides, it was Laura's idea."

"It was?" Alice's shoulders slumped. "Jack would never—"

"Jack's a policeman." Ruby took Alice by the hand and pulled her to the front door. "They do this all the time. And you want to make a good impression on your boyfriend's mother, right?"

"I don't know…"

"You're just nervous. It's normal. Deep breaths." Ruby rang the doorbell. "Laura will be over the moon if you help with this."

"It's sure to send Jack into orbit," Alice muttered.

The door opened, and a beautiful older woman stopped short. She wore a Chanel suit, long pearls, and sling-back heels. She looked as though she were headed to a fancy luncheon.

"Oh, it's you. Is this her?" She pursed her mauve-painted lips as she sized Alice up, looking her over like someone considering buying a vacuum cleaner.

Ruby smiled warmly. "Well, isn't this a wonderful coincidence." She wrapped her arm around Alice's shoulders. "Laura's future daughter-in-law here recently decided to start a new cleaning service, and she's actively looking for customers."

Alice almost fell off the step.

Janet eyed Alice as she drummed her French-manicured nails against the glass top of the entry table. "You have a cleaning business?"

"She's an entrepreneur." Ruby rubbed Alice's back. "Janet, this is Alice. Alice, this is Janet."

"*Mrs.* Ferguson," Janet corrected. "Is it just you, or do you have your own crew?"

"Just Alice." Ginny squeezed Alice's shoulder. "But she's quite capable."

"A little dynamo. You wouldn't believe it. She's like a mini cleaning tornado." Ruby swirled her hand to mimic a rotating funnel cloud.

"Do you have references?"

Alice opened her mouth, but Ruby spoke. "I can get you a list, but the proof's in the pudding. It's also guaranteed."

"Guaranteed?" Janet repeated suspiciously.

"One hundred percent. And the first cleaning is free."

Janet pursed her lips, and her eyes widened. "Well, I'd be willing to give that a try." She held up a hand. "Just on an exploratory basis, of course. When can you start?"

"Right now." Ruby prodded Alice forward.

Janet frowned.

"You did say you were hoping to get your house cleaned today. Well, now you can." Ruby held out both hands toward Alice as if she was the prize and Janet was the big winner.

"I do have company coming tonight for dinner." Janet eyed Alice again. "Do you need to change before you get started?"

"Oh, no." Ruby moved Alice forward and took a step back. "She's ready to go."

Alice stood there, stunned. She didn't know how to get out of this situation, or whether she should even try. She knew Jack would be mad, but the last thing she wanted to do was disappoint his mother.

"And the first cleaning is free?" Janet tapped her expensive-looking shoe on the travertine floor.

"One hundred percent." Ruby smiled, and she and Ginny took another step back.

Alice's heart sank. Like a child dropped off on the first day at school, she felt abandoned. She stepped toward Ruby and felt her arms rising, silently pleading with them not to go.

Ruby gave her a quick hug, kissed her cheek, and whispered, "Find the ugly cat." As she walked away, Ruby called back, "Alice, just give me a call when you're done, and I'll come get you."

This is not happening...

Janet held the door open. "Well. You don't have much time, and it's a rather large home, so no dawdling."

Janet snapped her fingers, and Alice jumped as if she'd snapped a whip.

24

DIGGING

Jack sat in the kitchen. The glow from Alice's laptop spilled across the table. He found himself jumping at every noise, expecting Alice to walk in on him at any moment. He hated sneaking around behind her back, but he wasn't ready to talk to her yet about what Amanda had told him.

He pulled up the website for *Enterprise News*, the local newspaper that covered Westford at the time of the accident. He'd had to pay a subscription fee, but now he had access to the digitized archives. The clacking of his keys echoed off the tile floor as he typed out his search.

As the "search in progress" wheel slowly spun, so did Jack's head. He knew what Alice had already been through. Having to revisit those memories was the *last* thing he wanted for her. But if their roles were reversed, he'd want her to do the same thing for him.

The spinning wheel disappeared, and the results filled the page. Jack scrolled through them until he found exactly what he was looking for.

FOUR KILLED IN CRASH.

Jack clicked the link, and his throat tightened when he saw the photo that accompanied the article. He'd been a first responder to many accident scenes, but this one was particularly brutal. A heavy-duty dump truck had slammed into Alice's family's car head-on. *The car's completely crushed. How could Alice possibly have survived this wreck?* Jack couldn't even tell what kind of car it had been. Rocks from the dump truck littered the roadway.

The truck hadn't suffered nearly as much damage. The front grille was covered with a wraparound metal fender that had been smashed in, crumpling the hood, but the truck looked drivable.

Jack read the brief article.

> *Four members of a Fairfield family were killed in a head-on collision on Route 128 just south of the Westford Split on Tuesday morning.*
>
> *The Westford Sheriff Department Accident Reconstruction Team is investigating. It is believed that the driver of the truck crossed the center line and struck the car, killing four of its occupants. Officials confirmed that the driver of the truck fled the scene after the accident, and police are actively searching for the*

suspect. Anyone with information is asked to contact the Westford Sheriff Department.

One family member, a minor child, survived and is in the hospital in a stable condition. Names are not being released pending notification of the next of kin.

Jack tried several other searches, but the short article was the only thing he was able to find. He couldn't even locate an obituary. He closed the laptop and slipped outside, the warm air wrapping around him.

He pulled out his phone and called the one person he knew who could get him the information he needed.

"Hello?"

"Detective Clark?" Jack said.

"How are you, *Stratton*?"

Jack grinned. He couldn't help it. Clark always stretched out his last name in a voice that made you think he chewed rocks.

"I'm good, sir. And you?"

"Still breathing. How's your old man?"

"He's good. I'm actually here in Florida visiting him. I'm calling about an old case in Westford. Thirteen years ago, a family of four was killed in a head-on collision with a dump truck."

"I remember it, but I didn't work it. I'm not familiar with the conclusion. Did they close it?"

"No, sir. That's the reason I'm calling. Do you know anyone in Westford who would have worked the case?"

"I'll have to ask around, but I knew a few guys over there. It might take me some time to track them down."

"I would really appreciate it, sir."

Detective Clark sighed into the phone. "Can you tell me why I'm digging?"

"One family member survived the accident. She was only a child at the time, but she needs to know what happened to her family."

"I understand. That's only right."

"I really appreciate it, sir."

Detective Clark chuckled, and it rumbled like thunder. "Are you kidding me? I should be thanking *you*! I'm already standing up. Doing anything that even *smells* like police work gets my blood pumping."

Jack knew that feeling all too well these days. If there was one thing that he felt was missing from his life, it was being a policeman.

"Give me a few days, and I'll see what I can find out."

"Thanks again, sir."

25

BAIT

Jack stood beside the kitchen table, sipping a glass of iced tea. Ellie, Carl, and Laura sat looking up at him.

"Are you going to make us wait all day?" Ellie wrung her gnarled hands. "What have you found out?"

"He just started this morning, Ellie." Carl leaned back in his chair. "Give the poor guy at least a day."

"Can we do anything to help?" Ellie asked.

"Actually." Jack set down his tea and pulled the frog statue out of the bag at his feet. "I need a good place to put this."

"Cute!" Ellie smiled.

"Put it?" Laura asked nervously. "Is it for *our* yard?"

"Don't worry, Mom. It's not for your yard." Jack smiled at his mother. "It's bait."

Laura hopped excitedly out of her seat. "You're planning a trap!"

"A sting." Jack winked. "I reviewed Carl's excellent list and figured this is the perfect lure for our thief. It'll drive everyone crazy." Jack turned it on and waved his hand in front of its mouth. The frog started croaking "At the Hop."

Ellie leaned in for a closer inspection. "We'll stick that in someone's yard and wait for the thief to take it."

"Exactly."

"What do you need our help with?" Carl asked.

"Two things," Jack said. "First, we need to figure out the best spot to put the frog. I was looking over your list—"

"Actually," Carl interrupted, "it's everyone's list. All I did was compile it from folks' individual notes."

Ellie squeezed his hand. "You did more than that, but thank you for including us all."

Carl blushed.

"What about the Harrisons' yard?" Laura said. "They've never had anything taken."

Carl shook his head. "Their backyard is lit up like a Christmas tree. And they have Bella."

"Their Pekingese," Laura explained to Jack. "She's a little yapper."

"I think the Wilsons' yard would be perfect," Ellie said. "Ida just planted some angel's trumpet, and the frog would look absolutely precious there."

"He's not asking where it would look good," Laura said.

Ellie's brows knitted together. "But it's so cute. I like it. Will you get it back after you catch the thief, Jack?"

Jack nodded. "Sure."

Carl leaned forward, and the frog started croaking "At the Hop" again.

"How do you turn it off?" Laura asked.

"You don't!" Jack moved the frog to the counter and faced it toward the wall. "That's the beauty of it!"

"Don't you think the thief will know it's a trap?" Carl had to speak up to be heard over the frog.

"They might, but I'm hoping the bandit is as brazen as everyone thinks and can't resist the prize."

"Like the golden arrow for Robin Hood!" Ellie said.

"Exactly. So…where do you think the thief will strike next?" Jack asked.

They debated for another fifteen minutes before finally settling on the Johnsons' house. They were up in Massachusetts for the birth of their first grandchild.

"You said you needed two things from us," Carl said. "What's the second thing?"

"I think everyone should take a shift keeping watch. We can break it into four shifts."

Carl rubbed his hands together excitedly. "Another stakeout! When do we start?"

"I'll go over and set up the statue in the Johnsons' backyard now. We'll start keeping watch at sunset."

"Carl and I will take the first shift," Ellie volunteered.

Carl leaned close and whispered into her ear.

"Oh, wait. No, we won't." Ellie shook her head. "We want second shift. And Ruby and Ginny won't want first shift either."

"I figured I'd take the late-night shift," Jack said. "Is there a problem with the first shift?"

"Bingo night," Laura said. "They have this new speed bingo. It's really fun."

"How about Ted takes first shift?" Carl suggested.

"He loves bingo," Laura protested.

Carl shrugged. "He's not here."

"Ellie volunteered already," Laura pointed out.

"She took it back," Carl snapped.

"Are there take-backsies?" Ellie's nose wrinkled.

Jack waved a hand in front of the statue to launch another rendition of "At the Hop," hoping to stop the squabble. Everyone stopped arguing and looked at him.

"I'll do it," Jack said.

"But what about the late-night shift?" Ellie asked. "I don't think I can stay up too far past eleven."

"It's not fair if Jack has to do everything," Laura said.

"I'm fine, Mom. Really. Two shifts. No problem. And Alice will be with me." Jack paused. "Where did Ruby and Ginny take her?"

Ellie chuckled. "She's helping a friend."

"A friend of yours? I hope they didn't leave her alone with some weird old…I mean…I hope they didn't leave her in some awkward situation."

"They're helping Mrs. Ferguson," Ellie said.

Laura locked eyes with Ellie.

"When's she coming back?" Jack asked.

"Won't be long." Carl winked at Laura.

Jack caught the glances shooting around the table. "You don't have my girlfriend doing anything that could get her in trouble, do you?"

"I don't know *what* she's doing." Laura held up her hands as if she were surrendering.

"Technically, neither do I." Ellie made a face. "Ruby just said that Alice would be perfect to help Janet, but I don't know *exactly* what she'd be perfect for."

Laura patted Jack's arm. "I'll bet she's helping with her computer. I'm sure Alice is having a wonderful time."

Jack imagined Alice pulling off one of his mother's plans—and then ending up behind bars, waiting for bail. He looked at Carl, Ellie, and his mother in turn, hoping someone would spill the beans, but each one simply smiled. With a sigh, he went to the refrigerator to refill his iced tea.

"Don't forget, Carl, bingo is fifteen minutes early tonight," Ellie said. "They're electing a new treasurer for the Community Group Fund."

"It's so sad about Roy," Laura said.

Jack came back with his tea. "What happened to Roy?"

"Roy was the treasurer," Laura explained, "but he passed."

"They still haven't been able to reach his daughter-in-law," Ellie said. "She's traveling in Europe. That's all they know. He must have gone just like that." She snapped her fingers, and Laura flinched.

"It's scary," Carl said.

Ellie smiled thinly. "At least he got to enjoy himself before he passed. When I talked to him last, he was happy and tan."

"I don't know about that," Carl groused. "I was reading up on heart attacks. I'll bet that trip put too much of a strain on his heart. All that cruise food—nothing but great-tasting, salty, fatty goodness. They say a minor heart attack can go unnoticed. And traveling is stressful. He just got back and—"

"Nonsense," Laura interrupted. "They also say a vacation can do a lot of good for a person. It's relaxing. Calming. Besides, those studies…those doctors…" She set her teacup down with a clatter. "I'm going to check on Ted." She got up and left the room.

"Oh, Carl." Ellie frowned. "She and Ted just went on that same trip. That's all she needs to hear while they're waiting to find out what's going on with Ted's heart."

Jack's head snapped up.

Ellie put a hand over her mouth, apparently realizing what she had said. An awkward silence settled down on the kitchen.

Carl cleared his throat. "I'm sure it's nothing to worry about, Jack. They're just waiting to hear back—"

Ellie squeezed Carl's hand and gave a slight shake of her head, cutting him off. "You should let Laura tell him." She stood. "I'm so sorry. I shouldn't have said anything."

Carl put his hand on Ellie's shoulder. "We'd better go."

As they shuffled out of the kitchen, Ellie paused and took Jack's hand in both of hers. She looked as if she were about to say something more, but instead she just patted his hand and said, "I'm sorry."

Jack mumbled, "That's okay. That's fine." Right now, he just wanted to speak with his mother.

Carl and Ellie pulled the front door closed behind them just as Laura walked back into the kitchen. "They left? Is everything okay? I wasn't too harsh with Carl, was I? It's just..." She trailed off when her eyes met Jack's.

"What's wrong with Dad?"

Laura sighed and walked to the table. She sat down and gestured for him to take a seat as well. Jack's body stiffened, as if bracing for bad news. He stayed where he was.

"Mom... Is it that bad?"

She pointed to the chair and forced a smile.

Jack sat.

"I'm praying for the best. The doctors aren't entirely sure yet."

"What do they think it is?"

She drew in a long, deep breath as she picked up her teacup with both hands. She put it back down without taking a sip. "The doctors believe your father has an electrical issue going on with his heart. They want to run some more tests to be sure. These things can be tricky to figure out."

"Why didn't you tell me? And why hasn't Dad gotten these tests done?"

"We didn't..." Laura sighed. "I didn't even know the extent of it myself. A month ago, Ted started getting very winded on our walks. He went to his doctor and told me afterward that the doctor wanted him to lose a few pounds. He was supposed to change his diet instead of doing any rigorous walking. I didn't read between the lines, Jack. Your father was shielding me, and I missed it."

Laura sipped her tea. "Turns out they sent him to a specialist, but he didn't tell me until we were on the plane coming back from the Bahamas. He said he didn't want to spoil anything." She sniffed.

Jack reached out and held her hand. "What did the specialist say?"

"They wanted him to have an electrophysiology study done right away, but your dad decided to put it off until after we got back and after your visit."

"Are you kidding me? I can't believe he took that risk!"

"That's what I said to him. Your father said the risk he couldn't take was disappointing me and messing up your visit. He said that *that* would *break* his heart." She shook her head slightly. "Please don't say anything to your father."

"Don't say anything? About something this big?"

"You know how he gets."

"He's been running around with me. I don't want him overdoing it if something's wrong. When is he having the tests done?"

"He gets a cardiac loop monitor put on next week and will wear it for a month. It should shed some light on what they haven't been able to pinpoint. Having you here is good medicine for him, Jack. I think it's helping take his mind off it."

"I'm going to talk to him, Mom. You know that."

She patted his hand. "I do. I'm sorry you heard about it from Ellie, but I'm glad you did."

Jack's mouth opened. "How'd you know it was Ellie?"

Laura took a sip of her tea, but Jack could still see the little smile behind her cup.

"You didn't know it was Ellie. You just guessed. And now I told you. Ellie didn't mean to tell me, Mom. It slipped out."

"Ellie's got a heart of gold. They all do. But enough about all that. I want to hear some good news." She tilted her chin and smiled. "My son decides to come for a visit, and he brings his girlfriend along…" Her voice rose hopefully.

"Did Alice talk to you?"

Laura shook her head, and her smile grew. "I fished around, but Alice gave me the distinct impression she wanted you to be the one to tell me."

"I'll bet she did," Jack mumbled. "Well, you're right. I asked Alice to marry me."

"Oh, Jack. I'm so happy for you both!"

Jack shrugged. "She said no, Mom."

The little saucer bore the brunt of Jack's mother's teacup. "She *what?*"

In his mother's hard eyes, Jack saw the look of a fierce mother bear. "It's my fault, Mom. Alice—"

"*Your* fault?" Laura's eyebrows rose along with her shoulders. "Your fault? I don't think so. She said no? And to think I was starting to—"

"Mom, dial it back. She didn't say *no* no. It was more—"

"Was it a yes?"

Jack shook his head.

Laura squeezed Jack's hand. "I'm so sorry. I can't imagine you down on one knee, ring in hand, looking up at her—"

Jack squirmed. "Don't get so dramatic, Mom."

"I'm not being dramatic. That's horrible. It's supposed to be such a monumental moment. Think about all the planning you put into it. Picking out the ring, figuring out the most romantic place to ask her, writing down what you would say…"

As his mother's indignation rose, Jack felt himself falling deeper and deeper in a hole. "Mom, that's kinda why she said no. Well, it was more like, 'Do it over.'"

"Did you go overboard? Some girls get embarrassed by too much attention."

Jack shook his head. "I kinda went under-board, Mom. Seriously, I'm starting to think Alice may have had a point. In my defense, I thought spontaneous *was* romantic."

Laura shook her head as if she had water in her ears. "Please explain exactly how you proposed to my future daughter-in-law?"

Jack scratched his chin. "Well…we were at breakfast…"

Those four words were the last Jack spoke for the next ten minutes. His mother fired questions at him, to which he either only nodded or shook his head. After she finished her inquisition, she leveled a stare at him and drummed her fingers on the table.

"Mom, I—"

His mother held up a finger, cutting him off. But she didn't say anything.

Jack waited another minute before he stood. "You think I blew it. I get it."

"It's not unfixable."

"You're making it sound like it is."

"Well, it's not. She's here, isn't she?"

"Shouldn't you be getting her?"

Laura looked at the clock. "She might need a little more time."

"What's she helping your friend with?" Jack asked.

"I think I hear Ted." Laura headed for the door. "One second."

Jack got up and leaned against the counter. He felt as though he'd just given a deposition. As he waited for his mother to come back, he looked at the montage of photos on the refrigerator.

He zeroed in on a photo of him and his father, taken at his high school graduation. They both were dressed in the traditional cap and gown—Jack's dad because he was a teacher at the school. Jack's cap and gown were red, and Ted's were black. In the photo, they had switched caps. His father was grinning as if it was the proudest day of his life.

It's just tests.

26

LOOK, I'M INVISIBLE

Ted parked in the Johnsons' driveway.

"You're sure we can leave this in their yard?" Jack asked.

"They'll be fine with it." Ted waved dismissively. "They're friends. I'll ask for belated permission."

"Well, okay." Jack grabbed the frog statue and the colorful yard spinner. "I'll scope out a good spot in back. You can wait in the car."

"I'll give you a hand."

"If you're up for it."

Ted eyed him suspiciously. "Why did you say 'If I'm up for it'?"

Jack shrugged. "You looked tired when we came home."

"Because I *was* tired. I took a nap, if you must know. Now I'm good to go."

"Just asking."

They walked around to the back of the house.

"Are you sure you want to put it out now?" Ted said. "Bingo doesn't start for another few hours."

"I'm sure." Jack smiled. He carried the frog to a wide tree stump that stood about six inches off the ground. "This looks like a good spot." He set the frog on the deep-brown wood. When he waved his hand, it started to croak "At the Hop."

Ted spoke over the frog's chorus. "This was a beautiful mahogany tree. A hurricane took it out." He ran his hand over the wood. "The tree guys wanted to charge several hundred dollars to pull out the stump and roots. Bill said he'd rather let it rot, but I think the real reason he left the stump was he didn't want to let it go. It was one of the most beautiful trees I've ever seen."

Jack stuck the pinwheel in front of the frog statue. It spun and rotated toward the wind, which made the frog start croaking out its song again. After a minute, the song stopped, but as soon as the pinwheel started spinning once more, the song started up again.

"Okay…" Ted looked around nervously. "That's going to make the neighbors go crazy."

Jack smiled. "Exactly."

"You're trying to? Oh, you think this is like that solar-powered rooster."

"The rooster was the first thing stolen. I hope the thief finds the frog irresistible." Jack looked around for a good vantage point. The houses were spaced far enough apart to provide lots of visibility. He pointed to a spot three houses down. "We can park over there and keep an eye on the statue from the street."

Ted shook his head. "That's over a hundred yards. At that distance, I doubt anyone in Laura's book club would notice if Godzilla waltzed across the backyard."

"I can see it, and we only need one set of eyes."

"Look over there." Ted pointed to a five-foot-high hedge surrounding the air-conditioning units in the next yard over. "In there would be perfect. Watch." He slid behind them, and only the top of his head was visible.

"Dad, we can watch from the street."

"It's too far. Come here." Ted's hand stuck out of the bushes and waved Jack over. "It's perfect."

Jack walked over.

"I'm invisible!" Ted declared.

Jack had to admit that he couldn't see his father until he got very close. He stepped around the bushes.

"I could bring a lawn chair and book, and no one would know I was here," Ted said.

"The homeowner might notice."

Ted's smile vanished. "Not this one. It's Roy McCord's house. He had a heart attack a few weeks ago."

"I heard. Did you know him?"

"A little. We chatted a few times. Roy kept to himself. Seemed like a good guy. He was a vet. Marines."

At the thought of Roy's heart attack, Jack felt his own chest tighten. "Dad?" He exhaled slowly. "Dad, what's going on with you?"

Ted narrowed his eyes. "Did your mother tell you?"

"No. But I want *you* to."

"Oh, Jack. I didn't want to ruin your visit."

"You'd ruin it more if you didn't think I could handle the truth."

"I didn't want to worry you. Or Alice."

"Don't be so stubborn. I need to know."

Ted looked at the clouds for a moment. "You'll understand someday, Jack, what it's like to feel weak for the first time. But you're right." He punched Jack lightly on the arm. "A son should know what his father is facing."

Jack found himself planting his feet shoulder-width apart, physically bracing himself for the emotional impact.

"Well, most likely," Ted said, "I just need to lose fifty pounds. The doctors ran some tests and some of the results…" He held out his hand and tipped it back and forth. "My heart's been working too hard. Taking the weight off should lessen the strain. The doctors think there might be something else going on, so they're doing more tests to be sure."

"What do *you* think?"

Ted leaned against the air conditioner. "I think I had one too many Li'l Kimmie snack cakes."

"You didn't tell Mom? Or me?"

"I didn't want either of you worrying. It's probably nothing. But no matter what happens, we'll deal with whatever comes our way."

"Well, I'll admit this does have me a little worried."

"See? That's why I didn't want to tell you!"

"I know. I just…I just can't imagine life without you."

"There's no reason to. I'm sticking around. And if I don't, I have my will—"

"Don't talk like that, Dad."

"I have to. I don't want to, but I have to. Look, this is a part of the whole proposal thing that I think you still don't understand."

Jack started to protest, but Ted lifted his hand. "It's speech time, and I'm taking one minute. Time me."

Jack took out his phone.

"'Time me' was just a figure of speech, but fine."

Jack put the phone away. "I was just joking."

"Marriage is a doorway that's going to change everything for you, Jack. The biggest thing is, you're getting a partner. Your mom is mine. I need to watch out for her now, when I'm here, *and* after I'm gone. She always has my back, and I need to have hers. The dreaded word is coming up here…" He pointed at Jack.

"Responsibility." Jack leaned against the air conditioner next to his father.

"Responsibility." Ted smiled. "I won't inundate you with details, but I do want to take part of an afternoon and go over the estate plans with you."

"You're not going to die, Dad."

Ted chuckled. "Hopefully not right this second, but none of us gets out of this life alive. I owe it to you and your mother to take care of things. And *you* owe it to your mother to know what the estate plans are, and what to do when I'm gone—which will be a long time from now. Agreed?" Ted stuck his hand out.

"Agreed." Jack shook his father's hand.

Ted held up his hand, which was now covered in dirt. "Uh, you might want to wash your hands, Jack."

"What?" Jack looked down at the air conditioner, and realized he'd been leaning against a muddy spot. His handprint was just visible in the dirt. And next to it…

Is that a boot print?

"Are you okay?" Ted asked.

Jack didn't answer. His focus was now on the small window above the air conditioner. That boot print, below a window, set off silent alarms in his head.

The reflected sunlight on the screen faded as it neared the corner of the window. Jack reached up and felt the screen. The bottom half pushed in.

Jack took out his phone.

"Who are you calling?" Ted asked.

"The police. The screen's been cut. Someone's broken into Roy's house."

27

MY HOME

Alice finished wiping the glass tabletop with a paper towel. Her back ached and her mouth was dry.

Janet's heels clicked loudly off the tile as she marched down the hallway and strutted over to the table. She dragged one manicured finger along the glass and then held it up directly underneath Alice's nose.

"I see you're ignorant of the fact that you should clean glass with a microfiber cloth so that you don't leave any residue. I assume that's because your regular clientele have low standards, but those are not *my* standards. Clean it again—and this time, please use the proper supplies."

Alice chewed the inside of her lip. "Certainly, ma'am. Would it be possible for me to please get a drink of water first?"

"There's a faucet in the laundry room next to the supply closet. You are not to use the kitchen." Janet glanced at her Cartier watch. "You're incredibly slow. At this rate, concentrate on the living room. It will have to do."

Several replies came to mind, but Alice reminded herself that she was doing this for Jack's mother and bit her tongue.

She lowered her eyes and headed down the wide hall toward the laundry room. As she passed by the enormous gourmet kitchen, she struggled to picture Janet making use of it. The woman would never pick up a pan, let alone peel a carrot. Alice wondered whether the beautiful kitchen was just for appearances. In fact, the whole house had a museum feel to it. Each room felt more like a staged display than a place where people actually lived.

My home won't be like that.

Alice's vow brought a small smile to her lips. A few years ago, she didn't even have a home—and now? Now she stood on the edge of a dream coming true, and she wanted nothing more than to settle right into her new life with Jack.

Had she blown it by asking Jack to make sure that was what *he* really wanted? He loved her—she was sure of that. She didn't want him to feel obligated to take care of her. She wanted what was best for him, even if that came at her expense.

Alice pushed the laundry room door open and saw the sink. Of course there were no cups, nothing to drink from. She'd have to drink straight from the faucet.

When she turned on the water, the stink of sulfur made her nose wrinkle. She left the water running, and after a few seconds the smell dissipated somewhat. She cupped her hands, held her breath, and took a hesitant sip.

She immediately spat the water out.

It figures Devil Woman's water tastes like it's imported from hell. She wiped the back of her mouth with her hand. *All this grief, and no sight of that stupid ugly cat.*

The sound of Devil Woman's heels preceded her appearance in the laundry room doorway. She glanced down at her watch and then gave Alice a frosty stare. She waved her hand dismissively and stalked away in disgust.

Alice stomped out of the laundry room. Her blood was boiling now. She may not be a professional cleaner, but she had busted her back all day, going as fast as she could. She just wanted to find the cat and get out of here.

She yanked opened the supply closet and began digging around, looking for a microfiber cloth.

Then she jumped back in surprise. A pair of red eyes glared like rubies out of the darkness.

Alice took out her phone and smiled.

28

THINK LIKE A CRIMINAL

Jack sat at his mother's kitchen table and sipped an iced tea while his father paced the floor.

"*You're* the one who figured out it was a break-in," Ted said.

"They're just doing their job, Dad."

"But they're not going to let you even take a look inside?"

"It's a crime scene, Dad. And now it might be a murder scene. They'll have to call in detectives, process the scene…"

Ted threw up his arms in exasperation. "But you're a policeman." He was incredulous.

"Calm down, Dad. I don't want to see you get worked up like this."

"Oh, brother. This is what I was afraid of. You'd find out about my heart and now you start babying me. I know my limits. I can take care of myself."

Jack set down his drink. "Even if I were still a policeman, they couldn't just let me in. It's not my jurisdiction. Now sit down. Relax. Sip some of Mom's herbal tea."

Ted made a face.

Laura came into the kitchen. "Honey, you should have some water."

"You see?" Ted looked at Jack. "Babying."

Just then Ted's phone rang in his pocket, and he put it to his ear.

"Is that the doctor?" Laura asked.

Ted turned toward Jack and rolled his eyes. "No, it's not the doctor. Must have been a wrong number. They hung up." He looked at his phone. "Blocked number. Probably a telemarketer."

"Something's the matter," Laura said. "What is it?"

Ted pointed at Jack. "Our son figured out that Roy McCord's home was broken into."

"Roy had a heart attack. Oh! You don't think someone could have…" Her hand covered her mouth.

"They could have broken in *after* he died, Mom," Jack said. "A lot of crooks read the obituaries. They target the house during the funeral."

"They should get locked up for a long, long time," Ted fumed, his face and neck turning a splotchy red.

"Don't get upset." Laura reached for his forearm and patted it.

"Don't treat me like some Fabergé egg. I might be shaped like one, but I'm not going to break. And I will *not* be coddled."

Laura leaned a little closer and softened her voice. She whispered, but Jack still heard her say: "But you *like* my coddling."

Jack waved his hands. "I'm right here."

Laura blushed. "Do you think the break-in at Roy's is connected to the thefts?"

"We have no idea," Ted said, "because the police won't even let Jack inside the house to look around."

"That's not a problem," Laura said. "I know a way to get in."

Jack held up a hand. "Please stop thinking like a criminal, Mom. No more break-ins. No more trips to the police station."

"I didn't break into the first house, and I am certainly *not* thinking like a criminal." Laura waggled a correcting finger at Jack. "I'm thinking like a *detective*. And you don't need to break in. Just have Bernie let you in. Roy gave him a key, so everything's perfectly legal."

***

"Robbery?" Bernie Lane raised his thick eyebrows so high they almost reached his even thicker hairline. He leaned against his doorway while Ted and Jack stood on the porch. "That's a damn shame. I came home when the police were just leaving. Helen must have let them in, because no one asked me."

"Helen Miller? The community manager?" Jack asked.

"She's the only one with access. It's senior living, son. You never know if someone's coming out of their house breathing or not from one day to the next. Are you sure they robbed the place?"

Ted nodded. "We're positive they broke in. Jack noticed a screen on the back window was cut, and there was a footprint on the air-conditioning unit underneath it."

"Glad I've got a dog." Bernie stuffed the front of his shirt into his belt. He untucked the back in the process, but didn't seem to notice. "Damn shame, stealing from a war hero."

"Roy was a war hero?" Jack said.

Bernie nodded. "Didn't talk about it. But I saw all his medals one day, so I looked him up. He took a bullet saving a guy at the Battle of Huế. He was a good neighbor, too."

"Do you still have a key to Roy's?" Ted asked.

Bernie nodded. "I was going to give it to his daughter-in-law when she showed up, but they haven't reached her yet. I don't get what the holdup could be. Why do you ask?"

"We're wondering if you could let us in," Ted said.

Bernie's thick eyebrows knitted together to form one long woolly caterpillar.

"There's been a series of break-ins," Jack began to explain, but Bernie cut him off.

"You don't need to tell me. The bastard stole my cheese-dial."

"Your what?"

"My Packers cheese-dial. It's a sundial, but the gnomon is a slice of cheese and the dial plate is Lambeau Field."

"The gnomon is the piece that stands up," Ted explained to Jack. "Its shadow tells the time."

"I know, Dad. You taught me when I was a kid." To Bernie, he said, "What did the cheese-dial weigh?"

"The whole thing?" Bernie thought for a moment. "Twenty, maybe twenty-five pounds. 'Course, that's mostly the post, and they left the post. Just took the plate. That was probably ten, maybe fifteen pounds."

"Was it an expensive piece or—"

"It's a Packers cheese-dial! It's priceless!"

Ted cleared his throat. "So…you'll be able to let us in? Jack's a police officer and just wants to look around."

"Sure. I'll get the key." Bernie disappeared inside. He reappeared a minute later sporting a Green Bay Packers hat and a gangly poodle on a leash. The poodle ran out and sniffed Jack's legs. "Might as well take her out to do her business. She goes more in the middle of the night than I do."

"Thanks for your help, sir," Jack said.

As they walked over to Roy's house, the excited poodle danced around Jack. Jack had to keep stepping over the leash to keep from getting tangled in it. Bernie made no attempt to rein the dog in.

Bernie unlocked the front door and entered. Roy's house had the same layout as Jack's parents' home, except the living room was on the right instead of the left.

"What exactly are you looking for?" Bernie shifted his weight from side to side, crossed his arms, and looked as if he was second-guessing his decision to let others enter his friend's home.

"I want to see what's on the other side of the window above the air conditioner." Jack walked through the living room to the kitchen.

The living room was immaculate and orderly, as though someone had used a level while arranging each piece. The magazines were stacked in a perfect rectangle, the remotes were lined up in a neat row, and the books on the shelf were arranged alphabetically by the author's last name. No pictures on the walls, but a few stood on the table near the phone in identical hinged frames.

An old wedding photograph caught Jack's eye. A soldier had his arm around a girl, and both of her arms were wrapped around his waist. He was in his dress blues, and she wore white. As Jack looked at the soldier standing straight and tall with a protective arm wrapped around his new wife, he felt a shift inside. Seeing that beautiful bride beaming on her wedding day, he knew he wanted to see a smile like that on Alice's pretty face.

"I thought you wanted to see the window," Bernie called out, holding the kitchen door open.

Jack followed Bernie through the kitchen to an adjacent laundry room. The rectangular window, its edges now smudged with fingerprinting dust, was directly across from the door. Beneath it was an empty wicker laundry hamper. The washer and dryer sat against the right wall, and a countertop ran along the left wall.

Jack nodded. "Thanks, I got what I needed."

"What would that be?" Bernie scratched his head. "All you did was look at the wall."

"It's a narrow window, five feet off the floor, with nothing underneath it for the thief to hold on to."

"So?"

"That narrows down the list of people who could climb onto that air conditioner, fit through the narrow window, and drop to the floor."

As they walked back into the living room, Bernie muttered something, but Jack couldn't make it out.

"Bernie," Jack asked, "do you notice if anything's missing?"

Bernie scanned the room and shook his head, his white hair swaying like cotton in the wind. "Looks just like it did when I took the pictures."

"What pictures?" Ted asked.

"After Roy passed, I figured I should document what was inside. Just in case. You know how it is when someone goes. The vultures swoop in. Family you haven't seen in years and friends you never knew you had—all looking for something."

"Did you take pictures of the entire house?"

"Nothing fancy. Just a panorama of each room. I was going to send them to Denise. That's Roy's daughter-in-law. But the email bounced back. She got remarried and changed her name. Guess she changed her email too."

"The police will want to see those pictures," Jack said.

"What for?"

"They can use them to see if anything is missing."

"Oh." Bernie nodded. "I'll go print them out."

"Do you have them on your phone?" Jack asked.

Bernie nodded.

"We should compare them to the room here."

Bernie took out his phone and nodded at Ted. "You've got a smart boy, Stratton."

"I do indeed. Thank you." Ted stuck his hands in his pockets and rocked on his heels.

Twenty minutes later, Jack, Bernie, and Ted stood in Roy's bedroom. Jack pointed to the picture on the phone. "Wait a minute. That's different."

"The goldfish bowl is gone!" Ted stared at the empty spot on the bureau.

"Oh, I can explain that," Bernie said. "I watered Roy's plants when he was in the Bahamas. I had to feed the goldfish too. After Roy passed, I knew someone had to take care of the fish, and I didn't want to keep coming on over here, so I took the fish home with me. I was going to give them to Denise, if she wanted them. You don't think the police will mind, do you?"

"You don't have anything to worry about," Jack said. "But these pictures will be very helpful to the police. They'll compare them to the current scene. I'll send a copy of them to my phone."

Bernie snapped his fingers. "You should have Darius take a look at the pictures too. Darius knew Roy better than anyone."

"Is Darius a friend?" Jack asked.

"Best friends. They were in the war together. Roy took Darius to the Bahamas with him. Darius Davis. Lives in Ogden. It's about an hour and a half drive."

"You wouldn't happen to have an address or number for him?"

Bernie shook his head. "Figure he's in the book. Can't think there'd be more than one Darius Davis in Ogden. But if anyone knew Roy, it was him."

As Bernie locked up, and Jack and Ted got back in the car, Ted's phone rang.

"Ted Stratton." His father furrowed his brow. "You need a meeting over that? ... When? ... Now? ... We all need to be there? ... Even the *dog*? I'll need to call my wife. We can be there in twenty minutes. Thank you, Mrs. Miller."

He hung up and sighed loudly.

"What was all that about, Dad?"

"Lady."

29

DELAY OF GAME

Dixon pulled his baseball cap down lower and rang the Strattons' doorbell. This was it. Laura was home alone. No son, no husband, no guest, and *no crazy dog*. No one. He glanced up and down the empty sidewalk, grateful for the blazing sun that drove people inside during the middle of the day.

As he lifted his hand to ring the bell again, he noticed the bare spots where the screen door hinges had been. He recalled the sound of the wood breaking and the metal bending, and he took a step back from the door just in case.

The dog shouldn't be home. Auntie said they were all out of the house now except for Laura.

Still, he pictured the beast rushing down the hallway and took another step back.

The door opened. Laura Stratton cocked her head at him as if he were a little boy who had skinned his knee. He wanted to punch her in the throat for the condescension.

"Hate to bother you, ma'am, but I lost my nametag the other day."

"I'm so sorry. You think you lost it here?"

"Yes, ma'am. When your dog attacked me." He glanced at the yard and then back at her. "I checked the yard and my car with no luck. My manager went through the roof and told me I'd get written up if I didn't find it."

Laura's eyes grew wide. "That's terrible. What's your manager's name? I'll call him and explain everything."

"He's not a real understanding guy, if you know what I mean."

Laura scanned the entryway and looked down the hallway, but the floor was empty.

"When I saw your giant dog, I spun around and hit my nametag," Dixon said. "I remember hearing something bounce off the tile. Maybe I knocked it off and it flew under that wooden thing over there."

"The hall cabinet? You may be right. Let me check."

Laura walked over to the hall cabinet. She turned her back to him and bent over to pull the cabinet away from the wall.

Dixon stepped inside. He reached back and grabbed the door handle to push it closed.

Finally. Alone.

But just as he was about to close the door, footsteps sounded in the hallway, and an old lady appeared. She reminded him of a librarian. When she noticed Dixon, she stiffened.

Dixon hesitated as he assessed the situation. There were only two. One would scream, but it wouldn't be for long. Would it be loud enough to attract attention? There was no way they could outrun him. But how could he make it look like an accident? The car was still here. Maybe he could take them both and drive it into the canal. In broad daylight?

"What is taking you two so—" A large black woman came down the hallway, five playing cards in her right hand. "Why, hello."

Dixon forced a smile. "Hi."

"Sorry, girls." Laura straightened up with a slight grimace and turned back to Dixon. "I'm so sorry, but it's not here. I'd be happy to explain it to your manager."

Dixon stared at the three old women, and his hand tightened on the doorknob. *Three shots. Grab the package and…go.*

30

LEASH THE BEAST

"I've seen many visitors with dogs," Ted grumbled as he paced in the hallway outside Helen Miller's office. "Frank's daughter brings those awful poodles with her whenever she comes."

At the mention of poodles, Lady raised her head and Jack tightened his grip on her leash. "You can't tell Helen that."

"I'm not going to name names. All I'm saying is that other people do it, and dragging us down here is ridiculous."

"Don't go getting yourself worked up, Dad. It's not worth it. Worst-case scenario, we'll stay at a hotel a couple of nights."

"You'll do no such thing. This is all Gladys's fault." Ted stopped and kicked at a doorstop. Lady looked down and sniffed at the spot. "Seven times."

"What?"

"This is her seventh complaint. She complained that I left the trash can out at the curb too long. That I trimmed the bushes too low and left the garage door open for a whole afternoon. Which was absurd. The broom fell in front of the sensor when we were leaving, and the door went back up. It was only open for a couple of hours. The point is, she has it in for us."

"You can't be sure it was her."

"I can." Ted stopped kicking at the doorstop and looked up. "Each and every time she complains, she tells us she did. She wears complaints like medals of honor. There's a reason she's the most despised, most—"

"Dad!" Jack held out his palm like a policeman motioning stop. Lady looked up at him, concerned. "Dial it back."

"She spends more time spying than the KGB. She's trying to ruin our time with you and Alice. This time she's gone too far."

"It's okay, Dad. Maybe Helen will be a dog lover."

Lady wagged her thick tail.

Helen opened the door and began to step out of her office, but when she saw Lady, she stopped in her tracks. She glanced back and forth between the men and the dog and cleared her throat. "I apologize for having you come in, but we did have a formal complaint we need to discuss." Standing there in her Prussian suit with the steel-gray blouse and a serious expression, Helen looked all business.

"A *formal* complaint?" Ted's eyes narrowed. "Is this really necessary?"

"Please come in." Helen held out her hand to four seats positioned before a wide wooden desk. "Will the other guest staying with you be joining us? And what about Laura? I did hope to speak with all of you."

"I'll be sure to convey the information to Alice and my wife," Ted said.

"Certainly." Helen smiled. "Please take a seat, and I'll go get the file." Helen cast a nervous glance back at Lady, exited her office, and shut the door behind her.

Jack pushed back two chairs, making room for Lady to lie down between him and his father. He felt as though he and his dad were two kids in the principal's office.

"Great," Ted muttered. "She's not a dog lover."

"Dad, shh. And please let me do the talking."

A moment later, Helen carried in a sizable manila folder. She set it down on the desk. "I do want to thank you again for coming in so quickly." She sat in the leather office chair behind the desk.

"Is there a rule that guests can't bring dogs?" Ted asked.

"Well, no. Guests are allowed to bring dogs."

"Wonderful." Ted clapped his hands together and stood up as if everything was a done deal.

"But," Helen continued, "those dogs need to be on a leash and controlled at all times."

Ted remained standing. "Then we're compliant. Lady is on a leash, and she is controlled."

Lady's head jerked up. Jack patted her neck. Lady cocked her head as if she were listening to something.

Please don't freak out, dog. Not now. Please don't.

"Mr. Stratton, the question is really about the safety and comfort of our residents. The complainant is concerned that the dog presents a danger." Helen opened the folder and read the complaint. "The dog was not on a leash, was barking ferociously, and had to be physically restrained by hand as it made aggressive motions toward another guest."

"That other guest was Jack," Ted said.

Helen folded her hands on her desk. "And that's one of the reasons I wanted you to come in. I see that your dog *seems* very well-behaved, but it concerns me greatly if Lady did in fact turn against her owner."

"That's nonsense. Jack's her owner, and Lady loves Jack."

"Are you saying the dog didn't act aggressively toward him?"

"She wasn't aggressive," Ted said. "She was…just trying to get to Jack…so she…could comfort him."

Helen's eyebrows arched in disbelief, and Jack felt his own eyebrows doing the same.

Ted stood up straighter. "What if Lady was a support dog? I mean, because…she's bonded with Jack, who's a vet, and was simply trying to reach his side. They had just endured a very stressful plane ride, on which they were forced to be apart for the entire flight."

"Are you saying that this dog *is* a support dog?"

Helen's phone vibrated on the desk, and she picked it up. Apparently it was a text, and as she read it, her expression darkened. Her long fingernails clicked as she drummed them on the desk. "How long will your son be staying with you?"

"I don't see——" Ted started to say, but Jack cut him off.

"Just a few more days. And I just bought a new collar and stronger leash. I can assure you that we'll keep Lady under complete control. And I think your calling this meeting was very reasonable considering the complaint. You do, after all, have to ensure the safety of the community, and I'm sure you see that everything is, in fact, under control."

Helen pressed both hands flat on the table. She smiled, but Jack noticed the tightness around her eyes as she glanced back down at her phone. "That is a must. And I'm sorry, but if there are any more incidents involving Lady, then she will be asked to leave."

"I understand," Jack said. "You have my word. I'll keep her on a leash. Thank you for understanding."

"Of course." Helen seemed to relax as she stood and shook their hands. "It's only a few more days."

31

LOOSE ENDS

Dixon stretched out on the couch in the living room as he waited for his auntie to come home. He was in no mood to listen to her today. He had bigger problems.

A quick glance down at his phone made his throat tighten. He had another message, but there was no need to listen to it. Even though the caller ID read "Unknown," he knew from the Miami area code exactly who had called and what they wanted. He set the phone on the coffee table, screen side down.

The front door opened, and his auntie hurried into the living room. "You little turd," she fumed as she tossed down her purse and walked to the bar. "What sent you running back here without the package and your tail between your legs? She was alone, for goodness' sake!" She grabbed a glass and poured bourbon into it.

"No, she wasn't. She had her friends over—three of them. Did you want me to shoot 'em all and stick 'em in my trunk? If you do, I'll go and do it right now." He jumped to his feet.

"Sit your ass down. They're all back there now. We just have to wait."

Dixon held up his phone and waved it back and forth. "I don't have *time* to wait. I've got Miami breathing down my neck. I don't want them to think I'm double-crossing them."

"You're the supplier; tell them to wait."

"You have no idea the guys we're dealing with. They're psycho and would love an excuse to feed me to a gator. I have to get the package *now*."

Auntie finished the glass without taking her eyes off him. With each swallow, the disgust she had for him became more and more apparent. She set the glass down on the marble bar and poured another. "How did my sister ever end up giving birth to such a spineless wimp?"

Dixon stormed across the room and stood nose-to-nose with his aunt. He felt his lips pull back and the spit fly as he spoke. "Say it again! *Say that again!*"

Auntie's eyes narrowed. She raised the glass to her lips and sipped the bourbon. "Calm down. I've already figured out what we need to do." She pressed her hand in the center of Dixon's chest and pushed him away.

Dixon stomped forward. His arms shook as his hands balled into fists. If she weren't his aunt, he would have already punched her in the face. Still, backhanding her across the mouth was a delightful idea that he struggled to resist. "I need to get that package to Miami by tomorrow, Auntie. I'm not waiting any longer."

"You won't have to."

Auntie walked over to the armchair. She moved casually, but he could see the tightness in her jaw. He had made her nervous.

Crossing her legs, she motioned for him to sit on the couch. Instead, he walked up behind her and stood with his hands on the back of the armchair. "What's your plan?"

"I think this is a well that's run dry. We'll have to lie low for a little while."

Dixon winced as if she had slapped him. He was looking forward to that truck, and he needed a new engine for his airboat, too. Her announcement meant the money hose had just been shut off.

"However…" She swirled the last sips of her bourbon. "I know a way that we can have Ted Stratton bring the statue to us. Of course, you'll need to take care of both him and his wife. Is that a problem?"

"Of course not, Auntie." Dixon leaned against the back of the chair. "How?"

"Sit down, and we'll discuss it." She held her hand out to the couch. "Stop hovering over me."

Dixon leaned down and kissed her cheek. "You know how much I love you, Auntie. You have nothing to worry about."

Auntie reached back and stroked his cheek. "There is another detail you need to take care of. Our partner is a loose end."

Dixon walked in long, slow strides to the couch, sat down, and spread his long arms across the back. "Well, there's one thing you've always told me, Auntie. Never leave loose ends."

32

SWAMP WATER FROM HELL

Jack put Lady in Alice's bedroom and followed his father into the kitchen. Laura, Ruby, and Ginny were seated at the table, all talking at once. When Jack came in, Ruby jumped to her feet.

"It's gone!" she exclaimed.

"What is?"

"The frog," Laura said. "Ellie and Carl checked on it before going to bingo, and it's gone."

"Gone? It's still broad daylight. The thief wouldn't have stolen it in the middle of the day." Ted pulled a chair away from the table and sat.

"And from right under our noses!" Ginny added. "That bandit is brazen."

Jack scratched his jaw. "We'll deal with the frog later."

"But it's gone, Jack," Ruby said.

"I know." Jack turned to stare at his mother. "But right now I need to know where my girlfriend is."

"Alice?" Ginny said. "Is she still cleaning Janet's house?"

"Cleaning—?" Jack stammered. "You've got Alice *cleaning someone's house*?"

As Jack's eyes narrowed, Laura turned to gape at Ginny and Ruby.

"We thought we'd surprise you when Alice was done." Ruby's shoulders rose, along with her voice. She held up her hands. "Surprise."

"We did ask you if she could help a friend," Ginny said.

Jack groaned. "Cleaning a house is a lot more than helping a friend. Come on, Mom. This is supposed to be a relaxing visit with my loving parents. Where is this house?"

Laura hesitated. "We probably shouldn't go over there. It might raise suspicions. Alice will come back when she's through."

"We'll go get her in a minute, Jack." Ted turned to his wife. "I have the distinct feeling there's a lot more to this cleaning favor than your mother is telling us."

Jack folded his arms. "Oh, really?"

Laura tapped a hand against her chest. "I had nothing to do with this."

Everyone looked at Ruby.

Ruby gazed guiltily at her teacup. "I thought it was a sound plan. Alice said she had done undercover work before, and a cleaning company made perfect sense."

"There's clearly nothing sound or sensible about this plan," Ted huffed.

"Having my girlfriend go undercover as a cleaning agency isn't a plan," Jack said. "It's a recipe for disaster."

"It was Laura's idea," Ruby said.

"It most certainly was not." Laura sat a little taller in her chair.

"You always said you wanted to get a look around inside Janet's house," Ginny said.

"Mom," Jack said, "we had a deal. I agreed to look into the thefts, and you agreed to not take matters into your own hands."

"I said that to Ruby *before* our deal. Honestly, Jack, I didn't know. I would never ask Alice to go clean someone's house."

At that moment, the kitchen door flew open, and Alice stepped in like a gunslinger walking into a saloon. She took two steps into the kitchen, spread her feet wide, and scanned the faces of everyone seated at the table. Her jawline was smudged with dirt, her blouse was smeared with what looked like grease, and her pants had a bleach splash down one leg.

"Whose idea was it?" she demanded.

Ginny pointed at Ruby.

Ruby pulled Ginny's hand down. "It was both of us, and you know it! We both came up with it—but I thought Laura approved."

Alice waved for Jack to follow her to the sink.

"You can stop giving me that stink-eye look," she whispered as she reached for a glass. "It wasn't my idea to sell me out to clean for free. I just got used, and I am *not* a happy camper."

"You didn't have to go along with it."

Alice's green eyes flashed, and Jack took a step back. Alice pushed up the faucet. "Before you yell at me, at least let me get a drink of water. Mrs. Snob E. Vanderbilt didn't want me sullying her kitchen sink, so I had to get water from the laundry room. It stank like swamp water from hell. I tried holding my nose, and I still couldn't drink it." She filled a glass and gulped down the entire thing.

"That's the sulfur," Ted said in a fatherly tone. "It's pretty common in well water here in Florida. It smells like rotten eggs, but isn't harmful. We use a filter to get rid of it. What a day you have had. I am so sorry, Alice."

Laura stood and wrung her hands. "Can I get you something to eat?"

"I would *love* something to eat, Mrs. Stratton."

Laura cleared her throat. "What did you find out?"

Ted took Laura by the hand. "After."

"But we've been dying to find out," Ruby complained.

"She had the cat figurine," Alice said proudly. She scrolled through her phone and pulled up her photos. She enlarged one photo and held it out for everyone to see. In the back of a large utility closet, between an old vase and a statue of a dolphin, was a black cat figurine with red eyes.

Laura, Ruby, and Ginny all rushed over to look. "That's the cat! You did it!"

Alice gave them all high fives. "*We* did it."

"I knew she was lying," Laura said. "This proves it."

"Not necessarily, Mom," Jack said. "It *could* mean she lied. The statue was a gift, right? Maybe Janet didn't like it, and she lied to spare Ginny's feelings. But it's also possible she stuck it in the closet and forgot it was there."

"Look, its red eyes are glowing," Ted whispered. "I would have put it in the closet too."

Laura slapped his arm. "It's adorable!" She turned to Jack. "And if she was lying, that means she could be the thief. She lied about the cat to throw off suspicion."

"Was Janet home all day?" Jack asked Alice.

Alice grimaced. "Most of it. She watched my every move like a gargoyle. 'You should get that spot again. You're using too much spray cleaner. When you bring your own, you can use that much, but I bought that bottle.'" Alice shuddered.

"Was she home in the last hour?" Ted asked.

"I think she was there. The last thing she had me clean was the lanai, and she wouldn't let me back in the house."

"Then she's not the thief." Laura sounded disappointed. "She couldn't have stolen the frog if she was home all day."

"So who is the thief?" Ruby asked.

Jack smiled confidently. "Dad and I are about to go find out."

33

IT WAS A GOOD PLAN

"What are we doing here?" Ted asked as they walked up to Carl's front door.

"I need to ask Carl about his spreadsheet." Jack glanced at his phone one last time before he rang the doorbell.

Carl opened the door, and his thick eyebrows pulled together. "Evening."

"Hey, Carl." Jack smiled. "Do you have a second? I could really use your help; I'd like to run a couple of things by you."

Carl pulled his shoulders back and lifted his chin. "Sure. Come on in and have a seat."

He led them into the living room. It was similar to the Strattons', but Carl's decorating had a distinct Western feel: dark woods, with cowboys and horses emblazoned on everything from the furniture to the artwork. "Can I get you two anything to drink?"

"All set," Ted said as he and Jack sat on the couch.

Carl took a seat in the leather easy chair. "It's too bad about your plan, Jack. Ellie and I went to check on the frog statue before our surveillance shift started, and the frog had already 'hopped' the scene." He chuckled. "That was Ellie's joke. Maybe we can try something like that again."

"We don't need to." Jack placed his phone on the coffee table.

Carl shifted in his chair, running his hand over the faded leather on the arm. "But it was a good plan. I think, under the right circumstances, it could really work. Ellie and I are going tomorrow for something else to use as bait."

"I'm glad you brought up Ellie," Jack said.

Carl looked from Jack to Ted. "What about her?"

"She's the whole reason behind these thefts."

"What?" Carl's initial look of shock turned quickly to laughter. He laughed so hard that he removed his glasses to wipe tears from his eyes. "I'm sorry." His guffaws subsided into chuckles. "But you think *Ellie* is the mastermind behind these thefts?"

"I actually said she's the *reason* behind the thefts. *You're* the mastermind, Carl."

"What?" Ted said.

Carl stood and shoved his glasses back on. "Now, you listen to me, young man."

"Mr. Wilkerson, please sit down." Although Jack's voice was calm, there was no question that he wasn't making a request.

Carl sat down. "This is absurd. I've been putting more time into trying to catch the bandit than anyone."

"I'm sure Jack has proof." Ted gave Jack a strained, please-tell-me-you-do-have-proof look.

Jack tapped his phone on the table. "My girlfriend has been giving me some tech lessons. See, we have this enormous dog."

"I've seen it," Carl said. "It should be in a circus."

"She's a great dog. Her name's Lady. And Alice really worries about her. So she got Lady this special dog collar, and she got me this app for my phone. The collar's special because it has a GPS in it, so I can track where Lady is with my phone. Just in case she ever gets away."

Ted slapped Jack on the back. "That's why you bought that dog collar in the pet store. It wasn't for Lady."

"Nope. It wasn't. The frog statue is hollow. I taped the GPS collar in there." Jack pushed his phone over to Carl, who had gone noticeably paler. "Do you want to see where that statue is now?"

Carl slumped in his chair. He didn't say anything.

"Why?" Ted asked.

Carl shrugged.

"Ellie," Jack said simply.

Carl shook his head. "She had nothing to do with this."

"Actually, she did. Do you remember when Ellie said the bandit would come for the statue like Robin Hood going to the archery tournament to get the golden arrow?"

Carl nodded.

"It's a great analogy, but Ellie got one thing wrong. Robin Hood knew it was a setup, but he didn't go to the tournament to win the arrow. He went to win a kiss from Maid Marian. The arrow was just a means to an end. That's why you've been stealing things, isn't it? Ellie's *why* you did it. You like her, and these stakeouts of yours were the perfect excuse to spend time with her. But you needed a reason for the stakeouts, so…you created the reason. Isn't that correct, Mr. Wilkerson?"

Ted slapped his forehead. "Why didn't you just ask her out?"

Carl stared at his hands. "Ask her out? What am I, seventeen?"

"No, you're seventy," Ted shot back. "I would think you'd have learned a thing or two."

Carl slumped down even more. "I haven't asked a girl out since…" He thought for a moment and gave a sad sigh. "It's been fifty years. I was married for over thirty years, Ted. I haven't even been interested in anyone since my Christy passed. But…I like being around Ellie. I wanted to spend more time with her. I tried to talk to her, but I'm just no good at it."

"So you resorted to stealing instead?" Ted said.

"It didn't start like that. It was that stupid solar rooster. That blasted thing was driving me insane. It was literally waking me up at the crack of dawn *every day*. I asked Beverly to take it down, but she refused—so I took it."

"I think everyone in the neighborhood was glad about that," Ted muttered.

"They were." Carl lifted his chin and looked directly at Jack and his father. "They talked like whoever did it was the hero of Orange Blossom. And then the book club got involved. Once they started looking into it, Ellie wanted to catch the thief. She was so excited about it, and she asked me to help. We met at her house. She even made cookies. But when nothing else was stolen…"

"So you kept stealing so you could spend time with Ellie?" Ted shook his head.

"I tried to take only the things that people didn't like."

"Bernie Lane loved his cheese-dial," Ted said.

Carl pointed at the Chicago Bears clock on his mantel.

"You stole his cheese-dial because Bernie's a Packers fan?"

Carl nodded. "I was going to give everything back after…" Carl's eyes went wide. "I'm going to have to move."

"What?" Ted and Jack said at once.

Carl stood. He looked close to tears. "I have to. Ellie will be so embarrassed. I stole the dates with her too. She had no idea what I was up to. Everyone will know that I'm nothing but an old fool. Seventy years without as much as a parking ticket, and now I'm a criminal. A repeat offender! Are you here to arrest me? Am I going to jail? Don't go to the papers!" With his shoulders rounded and his worried expression, Carl suddenly looked a hundred years old.

"Just dial it back," Jack said. "You're not going to jail. Do you still have everything that you've stolen?"

"It's in my garage."

"Good. Now, I need to talk to you about the break-in at Roy McCord's."

"I had nothing to do with that. I didn't take anything from Roy's. To tell you the truth, Roy kinda scared me."

"I know you didn't break into Roy's."

"How do you know that?" Ted asked.

"Because I'm telling the truth," Carl grumbled.

"You do understand why your credibility is in question," Ted shot back.

"I'm not a liar."

"Dad, there's no way Carl climbed onto the air-conditioning unit, cut the screen, and pulled himself up through the window to get into Roy's house. But someone did. And I need to know if whoever broke into Roy's broke into anyone else's house. So Carl, I need you to go over the sheet and flag everything that you stole."

34

SURPRISE

Dixon waited until he heard the bathroom door close and the fan turn on before he got off the couch and hurried over to Auntie's purse. He'd already blown through his cash, and he wasn't going to be getting any more until he got the Strattons' statue.

Auntie had three hundred dollars in cash. *One for her and two for me,* he said to himself as he pocketed two hundred dollars. He'd make her an extra-strong vodka and hope she'd forget how much she had. He grabbed her American Express, too, snapped the bag closed—

And looked up to see Auntie in the doorway with her silver Glock pointed at his chest.

Dixon straightened up. "I was going to ask for a loan."

"Get off my rug." Auntie walked forward, keeping the gun trained on him.

"You can't be serious, Auntie. I only took fifty bucks. You haven't paid me, and I need…to get some food."

"You're using again. I warned you, Curtis. Now step onto the tile."

Dixon laughed. "You've got to be kidding me. You care more about this stupid carpet than your own sister's son?"

"Yes." Auntie stopped at the edge of the rug. "And if you had a brain in your thick head, you'd know how much more valuable that rug is than you are."

Dixon's mouth twisted into a snarl. "My mother always said you were a selfish bitch."

Auntie grinned. "I bet she did. Your mother was a stupid one."

"You take that back."

She laughed. "Get off my rug, Curtis, and I'll tell you something that you've been dying to know."

Dixon stared at his feet. He wanted to call her bluff—but *was* she bluffing? Would she really shoot him? Not over fifty bucks, certainly?

Dixon stepped off the rug. "Well." He lifted his arms out wide, the two cobras pointing to the Anubis on his throat. "What's the big secret?"

"You know your mother introduced me to Baldwin?"

"Not this freaking story again." Dixon rolled his eyes. "You can have the fifty back and I'll pay you another fifty *not* to tell me the story of how you and my mom were both stripping and some rich, horny guy took you away from all that."

Auntie's smile was oddly calm. She shook her head. "I left off the part about how your mother 'danced' for Baldwin before I did."

"So?" Dixon shrugged, but as Auntie's smile grew, he realized what she was saying. "Wait…" His jaw dropped. "Your old dirtbag husband was my *father*?" He tasted bile in his throat.

"Your mother was so stupid she didn't see the resemblance until you were ten. And then she made the mistake of telling me she was going to tell Baldwin and ask for money. I couldn't have that. Couldn't have my money going to some snot-nosed kid. And I certainly couldn't allow Baldwin to have an *heir*—other than me."

"So, what? Are you saying you killed my mother? Your own *sister*?"

Auntie caressed the intricately carved, gilded lamp on the table. "What can I say? I love my beautiful things. And now that you've made such a mess of everything, you're risking me losing it all. I warned you, Curtis. No loose ends."

"Like you'd survive going to prison. You won't shoot me."

"They'd never put me in prison. A poor old widow who shot her drug-addicted nephew?" She adopted a meek, helpless tone. "He broke into my home! What could I do?"

"You rotten—"

Auntie pulled the trigger.

The gun clicked.

Auntie's eye twitched, and she pulled the trigger again.

The gun clicked again.

Dixon's eyes brightened. He pulled something from his pocket and walked up to her. "Oh, Auntie, you should see your face! You look so disappointed." He snickered. "But thank you for sharing that secret tale of sisterly love."

He leaned close enough for her to feel his breath on her cheek. "Now let me tell *you* a little secret. My mother didn't raise a fool." He held out his hand. In his palm were the bullets he'd taken from her gun. "Surprise."

35

EMBRACE THE HATE

Jack pulled into the quiet park and Alice shifted nervously in her seat.

"I thought we were going to go talk to Roy's friend." She straightened up and unclicked her seat belt.

"We will. We need to talk first." Jack put the car into park but didn't shut it off. "It's not about the whole marriage thing."

Alice's fingers traced the plastic outline of the door handle. Like a teeter-totter, her shoulders slumped for a second and then rose. "It's not a marriage *thing*."

"Bad choice of words," Jack admitted. "Look, this is going to be tough enough as it is, and I'm already dancing on eggshells. But I need to talk to you about something else."

Alice turned in her seat to face him. Her right hand was balled into a fist. Jack knew it was a defense mechanism. She was nervous, so she'd shifted into self-protection mode.

"It's about your mom," Jack said.

Alice gasped slightly. Clearly, this was not a topic she had anticipated. She looked at Jack with her green eyes wide.

His words brought pain. He knew they would. Jack wanted to wrap his arms around her and stop this difficult conversation in its tracks. He didn't want to hurt Alice, but she had to know the truth.

"I realized that after your family died, you didn't have anything of theirs to help remember them by. The same thing happened to Chandler and Michelle, remember? They lost everything when their house burned down."

"That was something Chandler never talked about."

"He never talked to me about it growing up. But in Iraq…" Jack looked out over the grass and palm trees, but he saw another place, another time. "Chandler and I were on patrol. We came under heavy fire. The bullet missed my head, but the piece of concrete it shattered didn't. It hit me here." He tilted his head away and showed the jagged scar on the side of his neck. "I told you it was a battle scar when we first started dating, but I didn't tell you the whole story."

"Why?"

"I don't know. But no more secrets, right?"

She nodded and ran her fingertips over it. Her gentle touch stood in stark contrast to his memory of the pain.

"I didn't think a person could hurt that bad," Jack said. "Chandler dropped on top of me and applied pressure to the wound." He chuckled. "Between him crushing me with his body and jamming down on my neck, I thought I'd suffocate before I bled to death. With what little air I had, I kept screaming."

"You were in pain. It's okay to scream."

"Not when the enemy is close by." Jack held her hand. "You don't want to draw machine gun fire. But I just couldn't stop myself. We were waiting for the medic, and Chandler said something I never expected: '*Embrace the hate.*'"

Alice lifted her chin, shifting her weight toward the door.

"Freaked me out," Jack said. "Chandler told me, 'Don't run from the pain. Embrace it. Hug it, and then kill it. It ain't as bad as you think. But it's you or the pain. It'll kill you if you let it. Kill it first.'"

Sweat rolled down Jack's back. He reached out and redirected the air-conditioning vent toward Alice. "Blood was spraying out of my neck. I thought I was dying. I told him he didn't know pain like this. Chandler pressed harder and said—" Jack had to stop for a moment to swallow down the lump that had formed in his throat. "He said, 'I covered Michelle's ears so she couldn't hear my parents' screams as they burned to death. I covered her ears and couldn't cover my own. So, yeah, Jack. I know pain. It burned in me for years. It didn't stop hurting until I embraced the agony I was in. Embrace it, Jack. Face it, and kill it.'"

Jack took a deep breath. "Those were the last words I heard before I woke up in the hospital.

"We talked about it again after I got patched up. Chandler said that before he made himself face the pain of his parents' deaths, he felt like he was losing them all over again, because he was forgetting who they were. Somehow, by denying the pain, he had been denying himself the feeling of love for them too. But after he faced what happened, after he embraced the pain, the happy memories came back to him."

Alice let go of his hand. She planted both feet flat on the floor and her hands on her thighs, bracing herself for whatever Jack had to say. "What are you telling me?"

"I located a friend of your mother's," Jack said. "She had moved to Florida. I didn't want to tell you until I was sure, because I've been looking everywhere and striking out every time."

"You met her?"

"Her name's Amanda Holt. She's going to visit her sister next month in Darrington, and she said she'd love to talk to you then about your family."

Alice swallowed. "She remembers them?"

"Yeah. But there was something Amanda said that was different from what you remembered about the accident. I double-checked online and confirmed it. The person driving the truck that hit your family's car didn't die in the crash. The driver took off and has never been caught."

"No, that's not right." Alice turned away. "The other driver fell asleep at the wheel and crossed over into our lane. It was an accident. That's what the nurse said."

Jack softly placed his hand over hers.

"Did the driver fall asleep?" Alice asked. "Were they drunk? What happened?"

"I don't know. The newspaper article I found was only three paragraphs long and just said the other driver fled the scene. But I asked a friend of mine to try to get some details. And when we get back—"

Alice grimaced.

"I didn't want to tell you when we were down here, but I didn't want to keep it from you."

She turned to face him again. "I'm glad you told me. Don't keep anything from me, please?"

"I'm not. That's all I know."

She shook her head, and her green eyes locked on his. "I mean about anything. Always just let me know, okay? Promise?"

Jack pushed a strand of hair behind her ear. "I promise you, no secrets."

"Thanks, Jack."

"We'll find out what happened." He reached into the backseat and took out a bag. "Amanda had two things that she thought you should have."

Alice leaned away as if Jack held a bomb.

"Don't worry. This part is all good."

Back at the house, Jack's mother had given him a jewelry box to put the butterfly brooch in. He took it out now and handed it to Alice. "Your mother loaned this to Amanda. Amanda said it was your mom's favorite."

Alice held the box with trembling hands. "Is it...is it a butterfly pin?" Her voice was so soft, Jack barely heard her.

"Yes."

Jack expected her to open the box, but she held it to her chest, closed her eyes, and began to cry.

"My dad gave it to her," she whispered.

Jack's heart hurt seeing her in such pain.

She looked up at him. "You said two things?"

Jack took out the framed photo.

Alice drew in a ragged breath. A storm of emotions crossed her face, and her whole body began to tremble. Jack wrapped an arm around her, and she collapsed against him, putting her head against his chest. She quietly sobbed, and he rocked her back and forth while her tears softly fell.

They stayed like that for a long time.

36

OLD FRIENDS

"Did you serve with Roy?" Jack asked the elderly soldier sitting across from him.

Jack and Alice were squeezed onto a worn loveseat covered with a tattered woolen throw. Darius Davis sat in a rocker facing them. The old man adjusted his thick glasses and leaned against the arm of the chair. "We were in the same theater, but that's really the extent. I had it easy. I was just a radio operator. In Laos."

"What branch?" Jack asked.

"Army. Roy was a marine. Combat marine." Darius's trembling hand held out his phone. "I took a picture of his Distinguished Service Star to show to my grandson. He was doing a report for school."

"Did you know Roy well?"

Darius nodded. "VFW. Fewer and fewer of us old veterans nowadays. Roy was a good man. Not a bragger. He didn't talk about the war much. Damn shame. Dies alone, and someone goes and breaks into his home."

"That's the reason we're here, sir."

"I don't know how I can be of any help with that."

"I have some pictures of the inside of Roy's house that I was hoping you might take a look at." Jack brought the pictures up on his phone.

Darius leaned back and made a face. "Sure, but I don't know how that'll be any help."

"After Roy passed, a neighbor took photos of the house's interior to send to Roy's daughter-in-law," Alice explained.

"And we're hoping that you could take a look at them and try to recall if anything is missing," Jack added.

"Missing? Ain't no way I could tell you if something was. I've never been in Roy's house."

Jack and Alice exchanged a quick, puzzled glance. "I just assumed because you're friends that you'd been there." Jack said.

"Sure, we were friends, but I've never been to his house and he's never been to mine. It's over an hour and a quarter ride, so we always did a meet in the middle. You know? Either the VFW or the Breakfast Connection on Old Minot Road. They have the best pancakes in Florida."

Jack made a mental note of it, not for the case, but to later share the glowing review with his pancake-loving father.

"Didn't you go to the Bahamas with him recently?" Alice said.

"I did, but we met at the airport."

Jack picked up the coffee Darius had given him. He stared down at the cup and considered where his questioning should go now. "Can you tell me about the trip?"

"Roy won it." Darius grinned. "He was all excited about it at the VFW when he told me. Maybe he'd had one too many, because he asked me if I wanted to go with him. Of course I wanted to go with him. Who wouldn't take a free trip to the Bahamas?"

Darius picked up his phone and squinted as he tapped at the screen. "My grandson got me the phone and taught me how to use it. Smart kid. Computer wizard. But everything's so dang small. I had twenty-twenty vision until I was fifty-seven, and then boom, glasses thick as biscuits. They say the memory's the first thing to go, but you know it's really the vision. And then the knees. Those went when I was around sixty-two."

He pulled up a picture and held the phone out to Jack. "That's us in the airport. A selfie, they call that. You can scroll through the rest of the vacation from there."

Jack took the phone and flipped through the vacation pictures.

"It was a great time," Darius said. "It's not like the two of us were closing down the bars, but it was still fun." Darius chuckled. "Close down the bars. Ha. We were in bed by ten almost every night. Played a little slots. Did some sightseeing. Overall, we took it pretty easy."

Jack scrolled to the last picture. It was a shot of Roy and Darius flanked by two women in floral dresses. One was holding a huge fruit basket, the other a statue of a silver dolphin.

Jack pointed at the statue. "Did you go to the Silver Dolphin Casino?"

"Sure did. Roy won the cruise and that included free chips at the casino. Beautiful casino. Clean. The buffet had great crab."

"Did you or Roy keep that statue?" Jack asked.

"Roy got the statue and I got the fruit basket. There were nuts and salami in there too."

"Did you see that dolphin statue in Roy's house?" Jack asked Alice.

"No." She took Jack's phone and scrolled through the pictures of Roy's house. Jack looked over her shoulder. After looking through them all, she shook her head. "I don't see it in any of the pictures."

"Would Roy have given the statue away?" Jack asked Darius.

Darius clicked his tongue. "I don't think so. Roy said he had the perfect spot for it. In fact, I asked for it, but Roy wanted it, and it was his trip. Said it reminded him of his honeymoon, which was also to the Bahamas. It being a dolphin and all."

Jack jumped to his feet. "Alice, can I see your phone?"

She handed it to Jack, and he pulled up the last picture taken—the photograph of the inside of Janet Ferguson's closet. The cat figurine that Ginny had given her filled the frame, but beside it, on the shelf, was a silver dolphin statue.

Jack held the phone out to Darius and asked, "Does this statue look like the dolphin statue Roy won?"

Darius blinked a couple of times and shrugged. "I think so, but like I said, my eyes are really shot. Sorry I couldn't be of more help."

Jack shook the old man's hand. "Actually, you couldn't have helped us more. Thank you."

37

LOVE-STRUCK

"Should we check with your mom first?" Alice asked.

"I'm just going to talk to her. Right now, we're not a hundred percent positive the statue in her closet is Roy's." Jack shut the car engine off.

"Seriously? It's a silver dolphin, for goodness' sake. It looks identical to the one in Darius's picture. What are the chances it isn't Roy's?"

"Okay, maybe not good. But I can tell you it wasn't Janet sprinting across the lawn the other night. And even if it is Roy's dolphin, who knows how she got it? I just want to talk to her."

"We could go to the cops."

"And tell them that you made up a fake cleaning company to gain entrance to her house?"

"Good point." Alice stuck her tongue in her cheek. "You know, Jack, I honestly thought your mother wanted me to do it."

"Please stop trying to impress my parents. They love you. Okay?"

Alice smiled. "What are you going to say to Mrs. Ferguson?"

"That you saw the silver dolphin statue when you were cleaning and loved it. I'm going to offer to buy it for you."

"That's good. That's *really* good!"

Jack rang the doorbell. "I figure it's not too much of a stretch for me to play the part of a love-struck boyfriend, now is it?"

Alice blushed.

They waited a bit, but no one came to the door. Jack rang the doorbell again.

"She may have gone out," Alice said. "She barely left the house when I was cleaning. Scared I'd steal the silverware, probably. I bet she has errands to catch up on."

Jack listened for sounds from inside the house, and heard a hum coming from the garage. "Do you hear a car running?"

"It could be the air conditioning."

"Could be." With Alice following, Jack walked around the house to the window on the side of the garage. He cupped his hand beside his face and peered through the glass.

Inside was an ivory BMW, its engine running—and pinned between its front end and the wall was the body of Janet Ferguson. Her upper body lay flat against the hood. She wasn't moving.

Jack shoved up on the window but it was locked. He smashed the glass with his elbow.

"You can't break in!" Alice still stood off to the side, and from her angle, she couldn't see what Jack had seen.

"Call 911 now!" Jack shoved the window open.

Exhaust fumes hit him full in the face. He turned his head to the side, took a deep breath of fresh air, and climbed through the window. The fumes burned his eyes as he pulled the emergency release rope on the garage door opener and heaved the garage door up.

Jack ran to the driver's seat, dropped the car into neutral, and rolled it back.

Janet's body slid off the hood.

Alice screamed.

Jack picked up Janet's limp body and rushed her outside.

"Is she dead?" Alice's green eyes were wide with fear.

An elderly man and woman hurried over from next door. As Jack laid Janet down on the grass, the neighbor woman knelt down beside her. "I'm a doctor," she said.

Jack was coughing so hard now that he was having trouble breathing. Alice was talking to the 911 operator, but with his hacking, he couldn't hear what she was saying.

Jack doubled over and tried to gulp in air, but could only take a shallow breath before coughing again.

"Breathe through your nose." The doctor placed a hand on his back and pushed his head even lower.

Jack coughed, shook his head, and pointed at Janet. "Help her."

The doctor rubbed his back. "She's dead."

38

LET HIM SLEEP

"Why can't we go in the house and show the police the dolphin statue?" Alice asked as they got back in the car.

"Laws." Jack clicked on his seat belt. "We told French all we know, and he'll give that information to the detectives. Then they'll work with it."

"But we know that someone broke into Roy's house, stole the statue, and gave it to Janet. And now she's dead."

"Which is why I want to go check on my parents."

"I already tried calling your mom. She's not answering."

"Can you try again?" The rental car bounced over another speed bump as Jack sped to his parents' house.

Alice dialed, and a second later she grinned. "Hi, Mrs. Stratton. Hold on, Jack wants to talk to you."

Jack took the phone as he turned in to his parents' driveway.

"Hi, honey. Where are you?" his mom asked.

"I just pulled into the driveway."

"Oh, be quiet as you go inside. Your father's taking a nap. I'm heading to the pharmacy to pick up a prescription the doctor called in." She paused. "Actually, I've already taken Lady out for her walk, so would you two like to come meet me and maybe grab a bite to eat?"

Jack could tell that she really didn't want Ted disturbed. "We're good, but is there something I can do? Is Dad okay?"

"His blood pressure's fine, but he's feeling run-down. I'm hoping some rest is what he needs most. Could you and Alice go do something fun? Please? That'll make both your dad and me happy."

Alice poked Jack's leg and whispered, "Tell her about Janet."

Jack shook his head. "Okay. Love you, Mom."

"Love you both."

Jack stared at the front door but didn't say anything. That feeling of helplessness was rising. His parents were getting older, and there was nothing he could do to stop it. Time was undefeated.

Alice took Jack's hand. "I'm sure he'll be okay. Why didn't you say anything about Janet?"

Jack sighed. "I didn't want to tell my mom about Janet when she's out driving. She's not the best driver as it is, and she'd freak out and race back here."

Alice kissed his cheek. "You're a good son. But you're still pale. Are you sure you don't want to go in and get some water?"

"No. I'm fine. But I can't sit around waiting for the cops to reach out to us." Jack coughed again, his lungs still returning to normal.

"Do you want to go back to Janet's house?" Alice asked.

"They'll be processing the scene for a long time. We need to go to the community center." Jack put the car into reverse, but kept his foot on the brake as he stared at his parents' house.

Alice squeezed his hand. "Don't worry. Lady's guarding him. He'll be fine."

39

IN ON IT

Jack and Alice walked right up to Tia's desk. She was on the phone, but she smiled and held up her index finger.

"Are you going to tell me why we're here?" Alice asked.

"There are three things that simply can't be chalked up to coincidence. One, both Roy and my parents won a trip to the Bahamas while playing bingo here at the community center. Two, in both cases, they were given a statue by the casino that was part of the prize. And three, on the night of their return, their houses were broken into—and in Roy's case, the gifted statue was stolen."

"So what are you saying?"

"I'm saying, someone is working very hard to send people from Orange Blossom Cove to the Bahamas so they can bring back these statues. There's something illegal hidden inside those statues, Alice, I'm sure of it. It's a very clever smuggling operation. What customs officer would suspect a vacationing senior citizen of being a smuggler? As soon as my dad wakes up, I'm going to get a good look at that gecko statue."

"So why are we at the community center?"

"We're here to talk to Helen Miller, the community director. Because in order to win that trip to the Bahamas, you had to get a triple decker at bingo, and my dad said the odds of getting it were like getting hit by lightning. Which means the games were fixed. And if you're going to fix bingo, you either need the player to be in on it, or…"

"You think Helen's behind it? Wow," Alice whispered.

Jack shook his head. "No, not Helen. In fact, the reason I want to talk to her is because I'm certain she's not involved. Bernie Lane told us that Helen has a key to every residence in Orange Blossom Cove. If she were involved, there'd have been no need for someone to climb through Roy McCord's window; they could have just walked through the front door. No, I think it's Marvin who's in on this."

"The bingo announcer? He looks a little nerdy. Do you think someone like that could really be rigging the games?"

"He gives out the cards and calls the numbers. If anyone is fixing the game, it's gotta be him."

Tia hung up the phone. "Can I help you, Mr. Stratton?"

"Yes. I need to speak to Mrs. Miller, please."

Tia's nose wrinkled. "I'm sorry, but she's gone for the day."

"I'm trying to get in touch with Marvin. The bingo announcer."

Tia smiled. "Oh. He's setting up for the next game." She walked around the desk and motioned for Jack and Alice to follow.

They entered the game room. The tables and chairs were all set up, but the room was empty.

"Marvin?" Tia called out. "Marvin?" She looked around. "He must be getting something from his car."

They walked outside, and Tia pointed at a red Corvette. The car's trunk was open, but Marvin was nowhere in sight. "That's Marvin's car. Where could he have gotten off to?"

"Pretty expensive car for a guy running games at the senior center," Alice said.

Jack walked over and stopped next to the open trunk. Inside was the bingo equipment—the hamster ball, the projector, and the screens. But his attention wasn't drawn to the car; it was drawn to the asphalt, where a dark red spot was quickly drying in the Florida sun.

"Is that blood?" Alice asked.

Tia gasped, and Jack reached for his phone.

40

THAT'S AMORE

Ted's phone played "That's Amore" and vibrated on the bedside table. He pulled off his sleep apnea mask, rubbed his eyes, and did his best to sound upbeat as he answered. "Hi, honey."

But it was a man's voice that spoke. "Listen very carefully."

Ted checked the caller ID. It was definitely Laura's phone calling. "Who is this?"

"Come on. You're a teacher, and that's the best you can do at following directions? I said *listen*." The man's voice turned hard. "I have your wife. I bet you're listening now, Teddy. If you ever want to see her again, you will do exactly as I say. Is that clear?"

Ted stood. "Yes. Don't hurt her. Please." His heart began to race, and his breathing quickened.

"That's more like it, Ted. She's fine as long as you do *everything* I say. Understand?"

"Yes."

"You were napping, but you're still dressed. Put your shoes on."

Ted touched his hand to his shirt. *How does he know this?* "Let me talk to my wife."

"There you go again, not following directions. So, you want to hear your wife?"

There was a pause, followed by an anguished scream of pain.

Ted gripped the phone. It was Laura.

"Ted!" she cried out.

He felt as if a fist had slammed into his stomach. He doubled over and grabbed the nightstand to keep from falling down. "Don't hurt her!" he yelled.

"That's up to you, Teddy. Are you going to listen now, or do you need more motivation?"

"I'll listen. I'll listen." He cradled the phone between his head and shoulder. His hands shook as he put on his shoes. "My shoes are on."

"Good. Now get the loaded nine-millimeter handgun you keep in the nightstand."

The thought of denying he had the gun crossed his mind, but Ted instantly dismissed it. Laura must have told them everything. How else could this man have known he was dressed and had been napping? *Dear God, what are they doing to her?*

He opened the drawer. Inside, Laura's gun lay next to his.

She hadn't told them *quite* everything. Apparently she'd only told them about the one gun. *Smart.*

"Do you have the gun?"

Ted picked them both up. "Yes."

"Put me on speakerphone, Teddy. I almost forgot. This way I hear everything you're doing."

Ted shoved the guns in his pockets and switched to speakerphone mode. "Okay. You're on speaker."

"Testing, one, two, three." The man laughed. "I know how you love numbers, being a math teacher and all. This here is rule number one! You're gonna love this. It's an if-then statement, Teach. *If* you try to call anyone or let anyone know what's going on, *then* I put a bullet in your wife's head. Do you understand this hypothesis and its conclusion?"

"Yes. Please…"

"Breathe, Teddy. Breathe. Just do everything I say and everything will work out. Now, go into the living room and get the gecko statue you got in the Bahamas."

As Ted walked into the living room, claws sounded on the tile behind him. Lady had come out of the guest bedroom and followed him. When Ted picked up the statue, Lady barked.

"Is that the freak dog?" the man yelled. "Stupid monster almost bit me."

Lady growled.

"You know what, Teddy? You got that gun, right? Shoot that mutt in the head."

"What?"

"You heard me. Shoot the stupid dog right in its stupid face. Shoot it now."

Ted looked down at Lady in horror. Her big brown eyes locked onto his and then glared at the statue cradled in his arm.

"Shoot the dog or I shoot your wife, Ted." The man shouted to someone with him, "Break her arm."

"No!" Ted screamed. His chest hurt. The gun in his hand shook. He couldn't shoot Lady. But they were going to hurt Laura. "Th-the windows are open," he stammered. "The neighbors will hear the shot. They'll call the police. You want me to bring you this statue, right? If the police stop me, you won't get it. Let me just bring it to you."

The man cursed. "Fine. Get to your car, Teddy. See? I'm a reasonable man. Get here and don't say nothing to no one, and you and your wife can go on your merry way. But *if* you try to tell anyone you're in trouble, *then*…"

Laura screamed.

"Stop! Please!" Ted begged.

"Go to your car right now and head north. Keep me on speaker."

Ted practically ran to the garage, and Lady trotted after him. He thought about leaving the door open and letting Lady run loose, but he couldn't do that to her, so he left her in the house.

He got in the car, set the statue on the front seat, and put his gun beside it. He took Laura's gun out of his pocket and tucked it in his belt behind his back.

He was drenched in sweat, and the pain in his chest was starting to spread, but he ignored it. He had to focus on rule number one: saving his wife.

41

PEDAL TO THE METAL

"Dad! Dad!" Jack burst through the front door of his parents' house, with Alice right behind him.

Lady ran to them and whined loudly.

"Your mother's not picking up either," Alice said, her phone to her ear.

Jack checked the garage. "Both of their cars are gone. And look." He pointed at the bare place on the mantel. "The gecko statue is missing."

"Did they break in and steal it?"

Lady pressed against Jack's leg. "Not with her here," he said.

Jack spun to face Alice. "My dad always has his phone with him. Can you tell where he is? Is there some app you can use?"

"I never turned that feature on for them. I have it turned on for us, but not your parents. He could be anywhere."

Jack thrust a hand into the air. "Wait! I know how to find him. If he still has that frog in his car…" He yanked his phone from his pocket and pulled up the app that tracked the dog collar hidden inside the frog statue. "Yes! He's on Hatherly Drive." He scrolled the map. "Looks like there's only swamp out that way."

Jack and Alice raced to the car, with Lady on their heels. They piled into the rental, Lady in the backseat, and Jack stomped on the gas.

"Call the police," he said. "Report a possible kidnapping."

Alice dialed. "You think someone's kidnapped your dad?"

"He wouldn't just wake up, take the statue, and leave." Jack sped up. "But I don't know why my mom isn't picking up either. She's worried sick about my dad. She'd answer her phone."

When the 911 operator picked up, Jack gestured for Alice to hand him her phone. "I need to report a possible carjacking," he said. "Suspect's car is a blue four-door Chevy sedan. Florida license plate AV145A2. Vehicle is heading eastbound on Hatherly Drive. The suspect may have an elderly couple with them. The male occupant has a heart condition—" Jack's voice became strained.

Alice was holding Jack's phone, monitoring the tracking app. "The car just turned south," she said. "It's heading down Cyprus Meadow."

"Suspect's vehicle is now headed south on Cyprus Meadow."

"We're sending a responding officer that way," the operator said. "Can you see the car?"

Jack was practically standing on the gas pedal, which was pinned to the floor. The little rental car was shaking. "Not yet."

"How are you aware of the vehicle's location?" the operator asked.

"I'm using an app to track it." Jack saw the turn ahead, hit the brakes, slid into the turn, and punched it.

Cyprus Meadow was accurately named. Swamp trees lined the road on both sides, and tangled vines hung from the branches.

Jack's hopes rose when he saw his father's car up ahead. "I have a visual on the car."

"I need you to back off," the operator said. "The police are on their way. Do not approach the vehicle."

Jack hung up and handed the phone back to Alice. Then, like a fighter pilot, he swung in behind his father's car. His father appeared to be alone. That was good.

Jack flashed his high beams, but his father didn't slow. The road was deserted, so Jack moved into the lane for oncoming traffic and pulled alongside his father. As he did so, Ted turned to face Jack. He held his phone up with his left hand and then pressed his index finger to his lips. He looked gray, sick, and terrified.

Jack felt as if he'd just jumped out of a plane. His stomach churned, his chest tightened, and adrenaline swept through every muscle in his body.

"What do we do?" Alice whispered. "Why can't he talk?"

"I don't know."

Jack looked back at his father. Ted's eyes were wild. Jack could tell his father was dying to talk to him, but for some reason couldn't.

The rear window of Ted's car rolled down.

"Take the wheel." Jack pulled Alice onto his lap and started to shift over beneath her.

"What are you doing?" Alice said as she shuffled over him and into the driver's seat.

Jack grabbed his phone from her lap, stuffed it in his front pocket, and climbed into the backseat with Lady, who reluctantly made room. "Get as close to his car as you can." He powered down the rear window.

"You're not thinking about doing what I think you are," Alice said as she pulled closer to Ted's car.

Jack motioned her even closer. Holding on to the window frame, he pulled himself up so his waist rested against the door and the rest of his body was out of the car. There was still over two feet of distance between the cars. Jack blinked into the wind and checked the street. It seemed to run straight forever, and there wasn't another car in sight.

He motioned for Alice to close the distance.

The gap between the cars shrank to less than a foot.

Please, God, Jack prayed quickly and then reached for the other car. He grabbed the other window frame and pulled himself forward. Asphalt rushed by underneath him, and for a split second his feet caught the window of the rental car. Then he shot into his father's car.

His father coughed loudly to cover the commotion.

A voice spoke from Ted's phone. "Knock off the coughing. You're making me deaf."

"I'm coming. Just please don't hurt my wife," Ted said.

Now it all made sense. But it was the last thing Jack had wanted hear. *They've got Mom.*

He grabbed the passenger headrest so hard it bent.

"Ted, don't come here!" Laura shouted over the phone.

"Shut her up!" the man yelled, and a moment later, Laura screamed.

Jack clenched his jaw and looked into his father's desperate reflection in the rearview mirror. *Pull it together, Jack. Keep Dad calm.* He pointed at his dad in the mirror, pointed to himself, and then gave a thumbs-up. It was the best "we've got this" reassurance he could muster.

Ted reached behind his back, pulled out a gun, and handed it to Jack. Jack took the nine-millimeter and quietly checked the magazine. It was full.

They passed a rusted metal sign that read *Big Adventure Airboats*. "You told me to tell you when I passed the airboats sign," Ted said into the phone. "Big Adventure?"

"That's the one," said the man. "You're almost there. Just do what I say and you and your lovely missus will be home before supper."

Jack texted Alice: *Someone kidnapped my mom. At least 2 men. Dad meeting them. Fall back. Call 911. Wait for police.*

"You're coming up to a turnoff," the man said. "I left the gate open. Drive down until you see the two buildings, then stop. Before you get out of the car, throw your gun out the window. That's very important. I've got another if-then for you, Teddy. *If* you don't throw your gun out the window, *then* we'll blow your wife's head off. I have never liked math so much."

Ted glanced back at Jack and pointed to the gun on the front seat, next to the gecko statue. Then he motioned for Jack to get low in the back.

He turned off onto a dirt road, and the car jostled them back and forth.

Jack typed on his phone, *Do what they say. I'll surprise from backseat*, and then held up the phone so his father could see. Ted looked at it and nodded.

Jack crouched down on the floor.

Ted started coughing hard and slowed down. Jack switched his phone to the camera app, and then held it up next to the headrest and used it as a modern-day periscope.

They were headed toward two sheet-metal buildings that appeared close to falling down. The building on the left was the size of a two-car garage, and the one on the right looked roughly like a ranch house, with a green sedan parked in front. A man in a baseball cap stepped out of the truck, while another man, wearing cowboy boots and carrying a pistol, got out of the passenger side.

A third man, in a black tank top, walked out of the doorway of the larger building behind the truck—and he had Jack's mom with him. He had an arm draped around her shoulders, the gun in his hand resting against her chest. In his other hand, he raised a phone to his mouth.

"Stop the car."

They're not wearing masks. Jack's mouth went dry. He knew exactly what that meant. A kidnapper who didn't disguise his identity had no intention of letting his victim live.

Jack's father stopped the car.

"Toss the gun, Teddy."

Before Jack could stop him, his father threw the gun out the window.

"Now drive forward."

Ted started coughing again—hard. The sound seemed to come from deep in his chest.

Jack scanned the backseat. Apart from the frog statue and a canvas tote bag, it was empty.

"Now stop the car and get out."

Ted parked the car.

"Dad, no. Don't get out of the car," Jack whispered. "They're going to kill you and Mom. I have an idea."

Holding his mother's compact gun, Jack rammed his hand inside the hollow frog statue. Then he covered the entire statue with the canvas tote. The frog statue was slightly bigger than the gecko statue, but at a distance it might fool them.

"Get out of the car, Teddy!"

"I have the statue!"

Jack heaved the rear passenger-side door open and got out of the car while holding his hands up. In his right hand, hidden by the tote, was the frog statue. In his left hand was his phone. "Let my mother walk to the car and you can have it!"

"I told you no cops!" Tank Top screamed. He dropped his phone, wrapped his hand tightly around Laura's throat, and pressed the gun against her head. She started crying.

"I'm not a cop!"

Jack quickly assessed the threats. Both men standing next to the truck were now pointing their guns at Jack, but the man in the baseball cap was the bigger concern. Judging by his overhanded grip and tucked-in stance, he knew how to fire a gun. Cowboy Boots, by contrast, held his gun gangster-style: one-handed, with the gun turned sideways. With that stance he'd be lucky to hit anything.

"He's my son." Ted got out of the car. "Please let her go."

"You broke the rules, Teddy!" Tank Top shouted. "*I'm* the one making the rules."

"You can have the statue!" Jack held the canvas tote higher and took two steps away from the car. "Just let my parents go."

Tank Top laughed. "Why the hell would I let you go?"

"The only reason to kill her is because she can identify you—because you were too stupid to wear masks. But that's pointless now." Jack waved his phone back and forth. "I'm live-streaming this. Your faces are all over the Internet now."

Tank Top went pale.

"What the hell?" Baseball Cap shouted at Tank Top.

Cowboy Boots swore.

"Drop the phone!" Tank Top shrieked. "Drop it now!"

Jack let his phone fall to the sand. "The cops are already on the way, and now they know what you three look like. You can go on the run with whatever is in this statue, but if you kill a little old lady, the police will never stop looking for you."

"You idiot!" Baseball Cap screamed.

"You'll get the death penalty if you kill her." Jack stepped farther away from the car and his father. "Just let her go, and you can take the statue and run."

"That's not happening," Tank Top said.

"What do we do?" Cowboy Boots asked Tank Top.

Baseball Cap pointed his gun at Jack.

"Take the statue. Please." Ted stepped forward. His legs were wobbly. He looked back at Jack. The corners of his mouth were covered in spit, and his face was gray. He grabbed his chest and sank to his knees.

"TED!" Laura cried. Her face was filled with pain. She looked at Jack, and their eyes locked. In that moment, Jack knew that it didn't matter to his mother that a gun was pointed at her head—she was going to try to do something to save the man she loved.

And so was he.

"Take the statue!" Jack ripped the tote off his hand. The plastic frog began to croak "At the Hop."

"What the hell is that?" Tank Top said.

Everything happened at once.

Jack pointed the statue at Baseball Cap and pulled the trigger. The frog shattered and fell from his hand. Jack aimed and fired two more shots at Baseball Cap. The man's head snapped back, and he slumped to the ground.

Cowboy Boots started shooting before he aimed. Bullets flew wide as he raised the gun, firing wildly.

Jack shifted his sights and aimed center mass. He hit Cowboy Boots twice, square in the chest, and he, too, fell to the ground.

It all took no more than two seconds, but that was enough time for Tank Top to shift his stance and respond. He wrapped his arm around Laura's neck in a chokehold and yanked her off her feet, using her as a human shield, and unloaded his gun at Jack.

Jack held his fire even as bullets whizzed by his ear. He couldn't risk hitting his mother. All he could do was sprint right, drawing Tank Top's fire away from Ted, and hope for an opening.

He didn't anticipate what happened next.

Lady burst around the corner of the smaller building, barking ferociously. Alice was right behind her, a broken rake raised over her head like a spear, screaming as she charged. And at the precise same moment, Laura chomped down on Tank Top's hand.

He howled in pain and stopped shooting. But he didn't let go of Laura. He dragged her back toward the door of the building. He ripped his hand out of her mouth with a scream, and blood spurted everywhere.

Jack couldn't believe it. His mother had just bitten off the tip of the man's index finger.

The gun fell from Tank Top's other hand. Laura twisted around and clawed at his face, and he shoved her away from him and lunged into the building. Jack got off one shot before the man slammed the door shut behind him.

Laura landed hard in the dirt. Lady leapt over her and threw her body against the door. She was barking nonstop, and her claws sounded like saw blades against the metal.

Keeping his gun trained on the door, Jack ran over and reached down to help his mother up. But she only raised herself to her knees before she lifted her head and screamed, a wordless cry filled with agony.

She was looking toward Ted.

Jack spun around and looked behind him.

Alice sat cradling Ted's head in her lap. His eyes were closed, and a pool of blood was spreading across his chest.

42

HELP OR GET OUT OF MY WAY!

One of the stray bullets had hit Ted in the abdomen, and his shirt was already soaked with blood. Jack kept one eye on the building as he dragged his father over to the back door of the car. He thought he had hit Tank Top, but he couldn't be sure.

As soon as he had slid his father onto the backseat, he ripped off his shirt and pressed it down against Ted's bloody abdomen. "Alice, keep the pressure on it."

Alice knelt on the floor and pressed down on the wound, but the blood continued to flow.

"Ted, you hold on," Laura said, getting in the back of the car with them. She squeezed her husband's hand. "We love you and we need you. Please." She bowed her head. Jack knew she was praying.

Jack whistled for Lady, who climbed into the front. Jack jumped into the driver's seat and hit the gas. As they barreled away, smoke began to rise out of the sheet-metal building.

Tank Top's destroying evidence. The cop in Jack wanted to go and stop him, but the son in Jack wanted only one thing: to get his father to the hospital.

Jack fumbled to unlock his phone as he drove off the turnoff and back onto the straight road. His hands were trembling and covered in his father's sticky blood.

"Nine one one, what is your emergency?"

"I'm transporting a gunshot victim, critical condition, with a cardiac history. Driving a green four-door sedan, Florida plates. I'm heading to—Mom, what's the hospital?"

"What?" she shouted.

"The name of the hospital?" he shouted back.

"Mercy Grove. It's on Marigold."

"Mercy Grove Hospital," Jack repeated into the phone.

Up ahead, three police cars with sirens raced toward them. The road was so flat he could see them from half a mile off.

"There are three cruisers heading my way. Tell one I need an escort to Mercy Grove Hospital. Notify the others that there is an active shooter inside the Big Adventure Airboats building—white male, six feet, black tank top and jeans, one hundred and seventy-five pounds, with a large-caliber semi-automatic. He may be wounded. Two additional shooters deceased. Possible fire."

"Can you repeat that, please?" the 911 operator said.

Jack repeated everything as the cruisers raced closer.

Ted was wheezing now. Blood gurgled from his mouth, and Alice started to cry.

"You need to stop and explain this situation to the responding police—"

"There's no time," Jack said. "My father's dying. I will talk to them at Mercy Grove."

"Ted," Laura said reassuringly, "we're getting you to the hospital. Hold on, honey."

"I have an ambulance en route, sir."

"He won't make it. Patch me through to the police."

"The police are ordering you to pull over."

The lights ahead stopped moving, and the police moved to block the road.

Ted started gagging.

Lady whimpered.

"Tell them my father will die if I stop!"

"You have to stop for the police, sir."

Jack kept the gas pedal flat to the floor.

"I have a medical emergency, and *I am not stopping.*"

Jack could see the cars clearly now. There were three of them, lined up across the road. Four policemen stood off to one side, while a fifth was jogging away from the cars carrying a spike strip.

"Please!" Jack shouted into the phone. "I can't stop! My father will die!"

The policemen ran for their cars. The one with the spike strip ran off the side of the road and waved at Jack. But he wasn't waving at him to stop. He was waving him on.

"Thank you! Thank you!" Jack shouted into the phone. "You need to make sure the firemen know about the armed man in the airboat building."

Jack swung onto the shoulder to get around the cruisers. The shoulder was a flat grass strip, but the compact rental was about as maneuverable as a golf cart. When the car's thin tires hit the grass, it felt as though he had driven onto an iced-over lake. They hydroplaned, skidding over the wet grass like a hockey puck, but Jack made careful, small corrections to the steering, and guided them back onto the road.

One of the cruisers was catching up to him fast. Jack rolled down his window and waved it up.

Sirens blaring, the cruiser pulled alongside Jack. The female officer in the passenger seat took one look in Jack's backseat and started talking into her radio.

Then she rolled down her window. "Follow me!" she shouted. "It's all construction, but stay right with me!"

Jack kept the gas pinned as the cruiser took point. They turned off the straight road and re-entered civilization.

"Ted!" Laura cried. "Ted!"

"He stopped breathing," Alice said.

So did Jack. Tears stung his eyes, and he wiped at his face with a bloody hand.

The road up ahead was clogged with construction vehicles, but the lead cruiser hardly slowed. It plowed right into the construction cones and sent them flying. Gravel pinged off the undercarriage as Jack followed. He could see the hospital ahead on the left, but a huge parking lot separated them from the emergency entrance.

Jack didn't care. He cut the wheel and headed straight for Emergency.

The car bounced over the curb, and they flew across the parking lot.

A group of emergency responders were waiting to receive them at the entrance. As soon as Jack screeched to a stop, they swarmed to Ted. Alice held Laura as Ted was loaded onto a gurney.

People shouted questions at Jack as they ran alongside the gurney into the hospital. Jack did his best to answer. "Nine-millimeter wound. Existing heart condition."

As they passed through the double glass doors, a doctor put a hand on Jack's chest. "Wait here."

Jack stood helplessly as they disappeared around a corner with his father. It happened so fast, he couldn't protest. He turned around to see the trail of his father's blood leading all the way back to the car.

Dear God, save my dad.

43

BENCHED

Jack sat on a bench in the hospital with his head in his hands, wearing the shirt from a set of hospital scrubs a nurse had kindly given him. He'd been in the hospital for twenty-seven hours now. His father had made it through surgery and been moved to the ICU. The doctors said the next forty-eight hours would be critical. Now every time he asked, the answer was the same: there was no change in his father's condition.

Everything since the shooting was a blur. At some point early on, Alice had left to take Lady home, and Jack and his mother had sat quietly, comforting each other, trying to keep each other's spirits up. They had both been interviewed by the police, and Laura had filled in the gaps about her kidnapping. Tank Top and the men had grabbed her when she was coming out of the pharmacy, she said.

Even though she'd been examined and cleared by the doctors, Jack was worried sick about her. After what she'd been through—what she was *still* going through—he knew she had to calm down or she was going to have a heart attack too. But she couldn't really relax until his dad got better.

And he *would* get better.

He had to.

Alice returned, and it wasn't easy, but she and Jack finally convinced his mother to go home and get some rest. There was nothing she could do at the hospital anyway. The police offered to have a cruiser stationed outside the house, and Jack promised to call the instant there was even the slightest development. He just hoped his mother could actually relax enough to fall asleep. She'd been through so much.

Footsteps came down the hallway, and Jack looked up to see Officer French and Detective Martinez approaching.

Detective Martinez had interviewed them last night. Martinez was young, but Jack was impressed with how sensitive he was when questioning Jack's mother.

Jack stood and shook their hands.

"I'm sorry about your father, Jack," French said.

"Thank you."

"Any update on his condition?"

"No change. He's still in the ICU. The doctors said he's a hell of a fighter. The bullet just missed his spleen, but the heart attack was major. It's touch and go right now."

"And your mother?"

"Considering everything that's happened, she's doing as well as can be expected. Thank you for posting the cruiser."

"That's why we're here, actually," Detective Martinez said. "We've recovered a body from the airboat building. It's badly burned, so we'll have to run a DNA test before it's official, but it's missing a finger, so it's gotta be your guy. You can rest easy. We got him, Jack."

"You must have shot him so he couldn't run," French added.

"It's still curious about the fire," Jack said. "If my bullet hit him, what started the fire?"

Detective Martinez shrugged. "There were fuel canisters all over that place. Maybe the guy lit one last cigarette while he was dying—maybe he stumbled into something…who knows. We'll let the fire investigators sort that out."

Jack nodded. "Thanks for letting me know."

"There's more. We know who the perp is. We ran his prints."

"How'd you get prints if the body was burned up?" Jack asked.

Detective Martinez cleared his throat. "From the fingertip your mother…*removed* from her kidnapper."

"His name is Curtis Dixon," French said. "He's the nephew of Janet Ferguson. We suspect he murdered her in her garage just before kidnapping your mother. The two other deceased shooters have an arrest history with Dixon, too. Three bad peas in a pod."

"Glad they're off the street."

"DEA is involved as well," Martinez said. "Dixon was smuggling black-coral heroin. The gecko statue was full of the stuff. Hard to detect. So you were right, Jack. They were using the bingo winners, including your parents, as drug mules."

"Did you find anything else in the airboat buildings?"

Detective Martinez shook his head. "Looks like it was just an airboat tours place, not a base of operations."

"What about the bingo announcer, Marvin?" Jack asked. "Have you located him?"

"Not yet," French said. "We're processing Dixon's house, and his aunt's too. But since we've got the three kidnappers, we'll be pulling back the cruiser from its post outside your parents' house."

"Thank you. I'll let my girlfriend know."

"Oh, and I've got a message for you," Martinez said. "I had to follow up on your background with Darrington PD—you know how it is—and when I spoke to Undersheriff Morrison, he said to call him if he can do anything to help. He said you're a good cop, sounded real concerned."

"I appreciate the message," Jack said.

"Well," said French, "we'll keep you posted."

Jack slumped back down on the bench and watched them go.

44

PROMISE

Laura Stratton fought back tears as she put together a bag of things that her husband would need when he woke up. She closed her swollen eyes and prayed for *when*, not *if*. The thought of losing her Ted was too much for her already throbbing head.

Alice knocked on the bedroom door and walked in. "Mrs. Stratton, can I help with anything?"

Laura started to cry again.

Alice rushed over and wrapped her arms around her.

"Thank you for taking care of my son," Laura said.

"Your son takes care of me, Mrs. Stratton. We're a team." Alice handed her a box of tissues.

Laura cradled Alice's chin in her hand. "It's been such a blessing, you coming into Jack's life. After all he went through as a child, and then losing Chandler..." She closed her eyes and her lip trembled. "We thought we'd lose Jack, too. He was falling away from everyone, and there was nothing we could do. But then you came along and saved him."

"You've got it backward. I've loved your son since the moment I first saw him."

Laura kissed her cheek and straightened up. "Thank you." She sniffed and wiped her eyes. "I should be with Ted."

Alice squeezed her hand. "Mr. Stratton will need you when he wakes up. You should take care of yourself now so you can be there for him then. Why don't you take a shower and have a little nap? If Jack calls, I'll wake you up, and we'll both head straight over there."

"I know I should rest, but...I don't think I could possibly nap right now."

"Okay then, I'll make you a deal," Alice said. "You lie down and at least try to sleep. I'll take Lady for a long walk. If when Lady and I get back you're still awake, we'll take you back to the hospital."

Laura nodded. "Okay. And you promise me you'll wake me up if Jack calls?"

"I promise."

45

CHAPEL

Jack stalked up and down the corridor. His head hurt so much he couldn't think straight. At least the case was over; he'd called Alice and told her about the police finding Dixon's body. She was safe. His mother was safe.

But his dad...

He tried not to scowl, but couldn't help but notice that every time someone walked past him, they gave him a wide berth.

Jack was dead tired, too. He needed another cup of coffee. When he reached the end of the hallway, he headed down the stairs.

Three vending machines sat in a little alcove, and Jack put his last dollar in the coffee machine. The machine hummed, but when he pressed the button, nothing happened. He pushed the button three more times and then started shoving the change return button. Nothing.

In a sudden burst of anger, Jack grabbed the machine with both hands and rocked it back and forth. He shook it so hard that he had to catch it from tipping over. He let the machine slam back down and turned away in disgust.

A little old lady coming out of a door just down the hallway stopped and stared at him. She smiled in a way that made Jack feel she'd offer him a cookie and a glass of milk if she could. She kept the door open and pointed inside.

Jack read the sign above the door. *Chapel.*

The woman held the door open. *"Mirar a Dios."*

Jack waved his hands. "I'm good. *Estoy bien.*"

The woman pressed her lips together and gave Jack a long look. In that moment, she reminded him of his Aunt Haddie. Aunt Haddie would agree with this lady. *At a time like this, God is just who you need,* she'd say.

Jack walked down the hall and through the door. The old woman patted his back as he went past.

The chapel was just a small room with several chairs facing a stained-glass window. It wasn't actually a window—it didn't face the outside of the building—but it was lit from behind and helped make the space feel less like the drab interior of a hospital. A table beneath the window held three electric candles. And as soon as the wooden door closed behind Jack, the bustle of the hospital faded into silence.

He sat down in the closest chair and leaned his forearms on the chair in front of him. He closed his eyes. He prayed a lot, but at times like this, he found it hardest.

He didn't know why. Was it because he was angry? Was it all the unanswered questions that he wanted to scream at the ceiling? Or did he just hate begging?

He was grateful that his parents were alive. Maybe he should start with that?

Thank you. Thank you for helping my dad. If you could...

Jack's eyes slowly opened. The words caught in his tightening throat. He stared at the electric candles and sighed. The LEDs flickered and moved, but it was no replacement for a real flame.

He hung his head and rubbed the back of his neck. He closed his eyes again and pictured real fire. But it wasn't candle flame he thought about. The fire at the airboat tours building still bothered him. *If it wasn't a base of operations, why would Dixon need to burn evidence? There would be no evidence to burn. And if Dixon was strong enough to start the fire, why would he not have been able to escape the fire?*

It didn't make sense.

Unless...

Unless he wanted to burn the body.

The hair on the back of Jack's neck stood up.

Jack remembered meeting Marvin and shaking his hand. And he remembered what Marvin said after: *Bingo ball bit the knuckle off.*

Marvin was missing a fingertip.

Jack ripped his phone from his pocket and dialed.

"Hey, baby," Alice answered. "I just took Lady out for a walk. Do—"

"Get back to my mother now. I don't think the burned body was Dixon's. Dixon's still alive."

46

YOU OWE ME

Dixon stood in the shadows of the backyard, glaring at the Strattons' house and cradling his mangled hand, which was in a crude bandage. He glanced up at the moon as it peeked out from behind the clouds and smiled. *Most of these crones should be asleep.*

As the moon slipped behind the clouds, his mood darkened. His focus shifted back to the Strattons' house.

She ruined it all. It's all her fault. Now where am I going to go? She made me kill Auntie. And she took my finger.

He'd been waiting back here forever. Waiting for his chance. The cruiser out front was gone now, but that wasn't what he'd been waiting for. He'd been waiting for someone to get that stupid mutt out of the house.

And now, finally, the girl had taken the dog for a walk.

At last, she's alone.

Dixon wiped his nose with his sleeve and walked across the lawn, carrying his hunting knife in his left hand. Its razor-sharp blade was a foot long, and the back of the blade had a serrated edge. He opened the kitchen screen door, popped a hole in the glass pane with the butt of the knife, then put the knife between his teeth like a pirate and opened the door with his good hand. The broken glass crunched beneath his boots as he slipped inside and closed the door behind him.

He listened to the silence. The thrill of being uninvited and undetected in someone else's house was always empowering. The fact that it was the home of Laura Stratton, the bane of his existence, made it all the more exciting. He'd come to set things right. He would make her pay for what she had done to him, to Auntie, and to his finger.

He licked his cracked lips, but even his tongue felt dry. He walked over to the sink and pushed up the faucet. He slid the knife in his belt, pulled down a glass, and filled it.

The water felt great on his dry throat. He'd taken the last of his black-coral heroin hours ago, and the stump of his finger was starting to throb again. He'd have to go through the medicine cabinet before he left. He'd have to get the PIN for the debit card, too.

He smiled down at his knife. It shouldn't be too hard to get her to give it up.

A door opened somewhere inside the house.

He deliberately left the water running. Then he strolled over to the kitchen table, sat down, and waited.

Someone was coming down the hallway.

Dixon quietly set his glass down and drew his knife.

"Laura Stratton, you'd forget your head if it wasn't screwed on," Laura muttered as she flicked on the kitchen light and walked over to the sink.

Dixon was immediately on his feet. "Shhh." He slid up behind her and held the knife to her throat.

She gasped but didn't scream. Her whole body trembled.

He loved it.

Moving the knife to her chin, Dixon slowly turned her around to face him. He held the knife in front of her and let the light gleam off the serrated edge. "You owe me a finger."

He should have seen the look in her eyes change from terror to determination. He should have, but he didn't. He was too focused on enjoying his moment, too secure in his own power and control.

So he was taken completely by surprise when his victim jammed her thumbs into his eyes and her knee into his groin.

Pain shot up into Dixon's stomach, but he managed to hold on to the knife. He raised it high, determined to drive it right into her skull.

She grabbed his bandaged hand and squeezed.

Pain unlike any he'd ever experienced ran from his severed finger to his groin. He dropped the knife and almost threw up. He screamed in pain and shoved her.

She landed hard on the kitchen tile.

Dixon's eyes watered so badly it was hard to see, but he had spotted the butcher block on the counter earlier, and his hand found the cleaver.

That stupid woman was trying to crawl away. He stepped on her ankle, hard, and she screamed. He twisted his boot, and she howled again. But it sounded wrong. It sounded like—

The kitchen door burst open, and the dog slammed into him. Dixon was thrown back into the sink, the cleaver tumbling from his grasp. He managed to shove the dog back, but her jaws clamped down on his ankle. It felt as though his foot was in a vise. The dog thrashed him back and forth, knocking him into cabinets.

He reached for the cleaver, but the kitchen door flew open again, and the girl—the one who was responsible for this stupid dog—charged in, screaming. She grabbed clumps of his long hair in each hand and started bashing his head on the tile.

Something cracked in his mouth. He tasted blood and saw a piece of one of his teeth on the floor.

He heaved the girl back. She slid across the floor with clumps of his hair still in her hands, torn from his head. He kicked at the dog and finally pulled his leg free, losing a boot in the process. Somehow he managed to scramble to his feet.

A salt shaker hit him square in the nose. Then a fork glanced off his cheek. Laura Stratton threw everything she could get her hands on at him.

Dixon turned and bolted out the door with the dog on his heels.

"Lady! Halt!" the girl shouted behind him.

Yeah, you stupid dog, halt, Dixon thought.

He ran as fast as he could out the back door and then cut to his right. He had run two backyards over when the ground dropped out from under him and he stumbled into a little inlet to the pond. Water splashed up to his knees. He cursed.

Those rotten bitches. All three of them. *Just you wait. I'll come back. I'll come back and I'll kill you all.*

He tried to scramble up the slippery bank, but slid back in with a splash. He looked down. The blood from his foot was turning the water red, and he could see little shapes scurrying away from him. Little shapes with long snouts. *Are those...baby alligators?*

Water erupted into a huge spray as the mother alligator burst through the vegetation. Dixon didn't even have time to think before she'd grabbed him by the thigh. She dragged him down, and the water rushed into his mouth, cutting off his scream.

Then the giant gator began to roll.

47

TUNA CASSEROLE

THREE WEEKS LATER

"**D**id you do that?" Jack asked his mother as he pulled the car into his parents' driveway.

Laura looked up at the huge "Welcome Home" banner hanging over the doorway. She shook her head. "Alice must have. That girl's a treasure, Jack." She gave his shoulder a squeeze.

The second he parked, she slid out of the backseat and hovered at the passenger side of the car. "Just take your time, honey."

"Yes, dear." Ted got out of the car very slowly.

Jack and his mom walked on either side of him as he went into the house.

Alice came to greet them with Lady at her side. Ted scratched behind Lady's ears and then wrapped an arm around Alice's shoulders. "Here are the girls who saved my wife's life."

Alice blushed. "I don't think she needed our help."

"One thing's for sure," Ted said. "Don't mess with the women in the Stratton family."

"Or the men." Laura kissed his cheek and squeezed Jack's hand. "Now let's get you settled before we talk anymore. We don't need to stand out here in this heat to chat."

"The doctor said I can putter."

"Putter *after* you get some rest."

"That's all I've been doing for three weeks, Laura. I can rest after Jack and Alice have left. Do you two really have to leave tomorrow?"

"I have a new job that starts in a couple of weeks," Jack said as they walked into the living room.

"He's going undercover." Alice beamed proudly. "On *Planet Survival.*"

"The TV show?"

"I'm not going to be on TV," Jack said. "I'm doing security."

After making sure Jack had a firm grip on Ted's arm, Laura hurried ahead to plump up the sofa pillows. "Undercover? For a television show?" she asked.

"There've been some threats made against the show, so the producers decided to beef up security. But they don't want it to be public knowledge. So don't say anything, please."

They all turned to look at Laura. Even Lady glanced up at her.

"Of course I won't say anything."

They helped Ted take a seat on the sofa, and everyone gathered around him. "Well," he said. "Let's see that picture."

Alice took out her phone and pulled up a photo. It showed Bryar and Boone standing over a twelve-foot alligator.

"It's enormous!" Ted exclaimed.

"I told you it wasn't four feet." Jack nudged Alice.

"I shouldn't have teased you." Alice slipped her arm through his.

"I can't believe that monster was living so close," Laura said.

"Are you talking about the alligator or Janet?" Ted joked.

"The alligator, of course. I know Janet was a wicked woman, but what a horrible way to go. Crushed to death by her own car."

"She got what she deserved," Ted said.

"Honey…" Laura said.

"I have earned the right to be upset about being used as a drug mule, having my wife kidnapped, and getting shot."

"But not *too* upset." Laura sat down next to him and took his hand. "How about some good news?"

"You made me some boots or a belt out of that gator?"

"No, dear. Carl and Ellie are dating."

"I take it no one found out that Carl is the Orange Blossom Cove Bandit?"

Alice giggled. "*Was*. He's officially retired, and everything was returned to its rightful owners. Anonymously."

Ted patted Alice's knee.

The doorbell rang, and Laura walked over to answer it. Gladys Crouse stood on the stoop with a covered casserole dish.

"Laura. I saw you pull in," she said. "Please let Ted know that I hope he feels better real soon."

Laura took the dish. "Thank you, Gladys."

Gladys turned to go.

Laura started to close the door and then hesitated. "Gladys? The book club is about to start a new novel. If you'd like to discuss it, we'll be meeting at Ruby's on Saturday at two."

Gladys turned around and eyed Jack's mother for a moment, as if she were waiting for a punch line. When none came, she actually smiled. "What are you reading?"

"It's called *The Girl Who Lived*. It's a mystery thriller."

She nodded. "Okay. I'll be there."

Laura shut the door and walked back into the living room.

"I think that heart attack affected my head," Ted said. "Did my wife just make peace with Gladys?"

"She extended an olive branch, dear. I had to accept it."

Jack smiled. "Technically, Mom, it was a tuna casserole."

48

HANGING WITH GOOFY

"**A**re you sure she's okay?" Alice asked as they strolled down Main Street USA in Disney's Magic Kingdom.

"She's fine."

"I can't believe Disney has a dog-sitting service."

"They needed a stable. I can't believe they took a dog that big."

"She's not *that* big," Alice said.

"She is too. They probably have her subbing for the Beast, or put her in *The Lion King* as a wildebeest. She'd be perfect for *The Jungle Book*."

"Stop it. Are you sure she's okay?"

"She's hanging with Goofy. That's Mickey's dog, right?"

"That's Pluto."

"Goofy's a dog, isn't he?"

"I think so." Alice squeezed his hand. "I still can't believe we're here. Where are we going first?"

They spent the entire day at the park, and it seemed like every few feet they had to stop so Alice could take a picture of Jack in front of some landmark. Several times, she tried to buy Mickey Mouse ears, but each time Jack shot the idea down. He picked up other odds and ends along the way for her, but not a hat. Soon he was carrying several bags as they made their way through the crowds.

In the evening, Jack surprised her with dinner at Beast's Castle. Surrounded by golden walls festooned with purple fabric, Alice chatted away in the glow of chandeliers. The flecks of gold in her green eyes sparkled and her delicate hands flew in all directions as she recounted her favorite moments of the day, but Jack spoke little.

Afterward, he walked her toward Cinderella Castle to watch the fireworks show. As they approached, he pulled Alice over to a quiet area.

"Let's watch from here."

"Okay." As Alice pulled out her phone to take yet another picture of Jack, this time with the castle lights sparkling off the water behind him, she noticed the time. "Ooh, they're going to start any minute."

"I hope not," Jack muttered. He checked his pocket for the hundredth time that day.

"What?"

"Nothing." Jack smiled. "Can you do me a favor?"

"Are you okay?"

"Yeah. Just wait here for two minutes."

"Sure. Why?"

"I want to get something before the fireworks start."

Jack started to jog away.

"You'd better hurry!" Alice called after him.

Jack broke into a fast jog. He didn't need to go far, but part of him was so nervous that he wanted to keep on running. He hurried around the corner, to where an older man in a driver's outfit, complete with top hat, stood holding open the door of a coach.

Jack jumped in, stuffed the bags in the corner, and frantically began changing his clothes as the driver moved the coach forward. Each clomp of the horses' hooves made Jack's heart speed up. At the rate it was beating, he'd be dead before they arrived. He checked and then double-checked that the box had made it from his jeans to his tuxedo pants pocket.

"We're almost there," the driver called back to him.

Jack peeked out the window of Cinderella's coach. He had no idea how Pierce Weston had pulled this off for him, but he was so grateful he had. Being a friend of the CEO of one of the world's biggest tech firms had its perks.

Alice was still waiting for Jack in the same quiet spot near the castle. She had her phone out and was taking pictures of the coach as it approached. From the smile on her face, Jack knew that she thought this was just more Disney magic; she had no idea he was inside.

Alice slowly lowered her phone when the carriage came to a stop in front of her. She looked back in the direction that Jack had run off to, and her mouth twisted at an odd angle. Jack imagined she was disappointed that he wasn't there with her to see it.

The footman jumped down and extended the stairs.

Jack took three deep breaths. He looked at the door as if he were about to leap out of a plane.

The footman opened the door.

It took Alice a moment to realize that it wasn't the park's Prince Charming coming down the steps—it was *her* Prince Charming. And as she gazed at Jack in his tuxedo, the wonder in her eyes grew.

Jack stopped when his feet hit the ground. Alice was beautiful. Her bright smile made him remember Roy McCord's wedding picture and the smiling bride. Right now, Alice looked that happy.

"She's waiting, sir," the footman whispered.

Jack strode forward and got down on one knee.

Tears appeared in Alice's eyes.

The footman stepped up next to Jack. In his arms was a pillow with sparkling red shoes on it.

Jack took the shoes. The footman gently took Alice's phone and began snapping pictures.

Alice's hand went to her mouth. Her whole body was trembling.

"I was going to do the whole Cinderella thing," Jack began. "But I thought a little twist on it was more appropriate. You told me once that your life was a little like Dorothy's in *The Wizard of Oz*. And that I'm like Toto, following you around. You were right. I'd follow you anywhere."

He slipped the ruby slippers on her feet.

"I'm no prince, Alice, but your father had it right. You're a princess. You saved me—not the other way around. From the moment you came into my life, you've been watching out for me. We both know life's not easy, and we don't know what's coming our way, but I do know that no matter what it is, we can get through it together. I love you, Alice, and I promise I always will." He reached into his pocket and took out the velvet box. His hand shook slightly as he opened it. "Alice Campbell…will you make me the happiest man on earth and do me the honor of marrying me?"

She stared down at the glittering engagement ring. Tears ran down her cheeks as she stood silently before him.

Then she bent down, threw her arms around his neck and kissed him.

Jack rose to his feet and cleared his throat. He lifted her chin, looked into her glistening green eyes, and moved in close. "I'm going to need an audible response to this question."

"Yes. Yes! Yes, I'll marry you!" She accentuated each "yes" with a kiss.

Jack gave a thumbs-up to the footman. A moment later, fireworks filled the night sky.

Alice started to cry again. Her shoulders shook. "I've been in love with you ever since you bumped into me on Aunt Haddie's porch."

Jack put everything he had into the next kiss. He was determined to give her the best kiss ever, but he wasn't prepared for the passion that met his own. Her soft lips sent a warmth right through him, and a peace he had never felt before.

"I love you, Jack."

Jack pulled her over to the coach, reached inside, and pulled out a set of Mickey Mouse ears. Two words were stitched into the back: *Just Engaged*. "Here's why I wanted to hold off on you getting a hat."

Alice kissed him again.

"And I have another present for you when we get back home. I'm buying you a gun and teaching you how to shoot."

"Really?"

"We're going to be partners, right?"

Alice nodded and kissed him again. "Alice Stratton. *Mrs.* Alice Stratton—even better." She giggled.

Jack rubbed the back of his neck and bit his lip. "Yeah. Sorry about that."

"About what?"

"Well, I figured that you were going to take my last name."

"Of course. I'm honored. Do you not want me to?"

"No, no—I do. I love you being Mrs. Stratton. It's going to take some getting used to, but it's great." Jack felt a smirk forming, and he tried to hold it back.

"Then what's the matter?" She pointed at his cheek. "Your dimple is showing. You're up to something."

"Is that my tell? My dimple?"

"That's one of them." Alice waggled a finger, but she was still grinning, and the fireworks made the green in her eyes sparkle. "Now what could be bad about my being Mrs. Alice Stratton?"

"It's your full name that could be a little problem." His dimple deepened.

"My full name?"

"Once you marry me, you'll be Mrs. Alice Samantha Stratton."

"Alice Samantha—" Her jaw dropped. "My initials spell A.S.S.! Jack Stratton! That is *not* funny." She swatted his arm.

Jack laughed and pulled her close.

THE END

THE DETECTIVE JACK STRATTON
MYSTERY-THRILLER SERIES

The Detective Jack Stratton Mystery-Thriller Series, authored by *Wall Street Journal* bestselling writer Christopher Greyson, has over 5,000 five-star reviews and over one million readers and counting. If you'd love to read another page-turning thriller with mystery, humor, and a dash of romance, pick up the next book in the highly acclaimed series today.

AND THEN SHE WAS GONE

A hometown hero with a heart of gold, Jack Stratton was raised in a whorehouse by his prostitute mother. Jack seemed destined to become another statistic, but now his life has taken a turn for the better. Determined to escape his past, he's headed for a career in law enforcement. When his foster mother asks him to look into a girl's disappearance, Jack quickly gets drawn into a baffling mystery. As Jack digs deeper, everyone becomes a suspect—including himself. Caught between the criminals and the cops, can Jack discover the truth in time to save the girl? Or will he become the next victim?

GIRL JACKED

Guilt has driven a wedge between Jack and the family he loves. When Jack, now a police officer, hears the news that his foster sister Michelle is missing, it cuts straight to his core. The police think she just took off, but Jack knows Michelle would never leave her loved ones behind—like he did. Forced to confront the demons from his past, Jack must take action, find Michelle, and bring her home... or die trying.

JACK KNIFED

Constant nightmares have forced Jack to seek answers about his rough childhood and the dark secrets hidden there. The mystery surrounding Jack's birth father leads Jack to investigate the twenty-seven-year-old murder case in Hope Falls.

JACKS ARE WILD

When Jack's sexy old flame disappears, no one thinks it's suspicious except Jack and one unbalanced witness. Jack feels in his gut that something is wrong. He knows that Marisa has a past, and if it ever caught up with her—it would be deadly. The trail leads him into all sorts of trouble—landing him smack in the middle of an all-out mob war between the Italian Mafia and the Japanese Yakuza.

JACK AND THE GIANT KILLER

Rogue hero Jack Stratton is back in another action-packed, thrilling adventure. While recovering from a gunshot wound, Jack gets a seemingly harmless private investigation job—locate the owner of a lost dog—Jack begrudgingly assists. Little does he know it will place him directly in the crosshairs of a merciless serial killer.

DATA JACK

In this digital age of hackers, spyware, and cyber terrorism—data is more valuable than gold. Thieves plan to steal the keys to the digital kingdom and with this much money at stake, they'll kill for it. Can Jack and Alice (aka Replacement) stop the pack of ruthless criminals before they can *Data Jack?*

JACK OF HEARTS

When his mother and the members of her neighborhood book club ask him to catch the "Orange Blossom Cove Bandit," a small-time thief who's stealing garden gnomes and peace of mind from their quiet retirement community, how can Jack refuse? The peculiar mystery proves to be more than it appears, and things take a deadly turn. Now, Jack finds it's up to him to stop a crazed killer, save his parents, and win the hand of the girl he loves—but if he survives, will it be Jack who ends up with a broken heart?

JACK FROST

Jack has a new assignment: to investigate the suspicious death of a soundman on the hit TV show *Planet Survival*. Jack goes undercover as a security agent where the show is filming on nearby Mount Minuit. Soon trapped on the treacherous peak by a blizzard, a mysterious killer continues to stalk the cast and crew of *Planet Survival*. What started out as a game is now a deadly competition for survival. As the temperature drops and the body count rises, what will get them first? The mountain or the killer?

Hear your favorite characters come to life
in audio versions of the
Detective Jack Stratton Mystery-Thriller Series!
Audio Books now available on Audible!

Novels featuring Jack Stratton in order:
AND THEN SHE WAS GONE

GIRL JACKED

JACK KNIFED

JACKS ARE WILD

JACK AND THE GIANT KILLER

DATA JACK

JACK OF HEARTS

JACK FROST

Psychological Thriller
THE GIRL WHO LIVED

Ten years ago, four people were brutally murdered. One girl lived. As the anniversary of the murders approaches, Faith Winters is released from the psychiatric hospital and yanked back to the last spot on earth she wants to be—her hometown where the slayings took place. Wracked by the lingering echoes of survivor's guilt, Faith spirals into a black hole of alcoholism and wanton self-destruction. Finding no solace at the bottom of a bottle, Faith decides to track down her sister's killer—and then discovers that she's the one being hunted.

Epic Fantasy
PURE OF HEART

Orphaned and alone, rogue-teen Dean Walker has learned how to take care of himself on the rough city streets. Unjustly wanted by the police, he takes refuge within the shadows of the city. When Dean stumbles upon an old man being mugged, he tries to help—only to discover that the victim is anything but helpless and far more than he appears. Together with three friends, he sets out on an epic quest where only the pure of heart will prevail.

INTRODUCING
THE ADVENTURES OF FINN AND ANNIE

A SPECIAL COLLECTION OF MYSTERIES EXCLUSIVELY FOR CHRISTOPHER GREYSON'S LOYAL READERS

Finnian Church chased his boyhood dream of following in his father's law-enforcing footsteps by way of the United States Armed Forces. As soon as he finished his tour of duty, Finn planned to report to the police academy. But the winds of war have a way of changing a man's plans. Finn returned home a decorated war hero, but without a leg. Disillusioned but undaunted, it wasn't long before he discovered a way to keep his ambitions alive and earn a living as an insurance investigator.

Finn finds himself in need of a videographer to document the accident scenes. Into his orderly business and simple life walks Annie Summers. A lovely free spirit and single mother of two, Annie has a physical challenge of her own—she's been completely deaf since childhood.

Finn and Annie find themselves tested and growing in ways they never imagined. Join this unlikely duo as they investigate their way through murder, arson, theft, embezzlement, and maybe even love, seeking to distinguish between truth and lies, scammers and victims.

This FREE special collection of mysteries by *Wall Street Journal* bestselling author CHRISTOPHER GREYSON is available EXCLUSIVELY to loyal readers. Get your FREE first installment ONLY at ChristopherGreyson.com.

Become a Preferred Reader to enjoy additional FREE *Adventures of Finn and Annie*, advanced notifications of book releases, and more.

Don't miss out, visit ChristopherGreyson.com and JOIN TODAY!

You could win a brand new
HD KINDLE FIRE TABLET
when you go to
ChristopherGreyson.com
Enter as many times as you'd like.
No purchase necessary.
It's just my way of thanking my loyal readers.

Looking for a mystery series mixed with romantic suspense?
Be sure to check out Katherine Greyson's bestselling series:
EVERYONE KEEPS SECRETS

ACKNOWLEDGMENTS

I would like to thank all the wonderful readers out there. It is you who make the literary world what it is today— a place of dreams filled with tales of adventure! To all of you who have taken Jack and Replacement under your wings and spread the word via social media (Facebook and Twitter) and who have taken the time to go back and write a great review, I say THANK YOU! Your efforts keep the characters alive and give me the encouragement and time to keep writing. I can't thank YOU enough.

Word of mouth is crucial for any author to succeed. If you enjoyed the series, please consider leaving a review at Amazon, even if it is only a line or two; it would make all the difference and I would appreciate it very much.

I would also like to thank my amazing wife for standing beside me every step of the way on this journey. My thanks also go out to Laura and Christopher: my two awesome kids, my dear mother, my family, my wonderful team; Maia McViney, Maia Sepp, my fantastic editors— David Gatewood of Lone Trout Editing, Faith Williams of The Atwater Group, Charlie Wilson of Landmark Editorial, and my writing coach Ann Kroeker, my consultant Dianne Jones, and the unbelievably helpful beta readers!

ABOUT THE AUTHOR

My name is Christopher Greyson, and I am a storyteller.

Since I was a little boy, I have dreamt of what mystery was around the next corner, or what quest lay over the hill. If I couldn't find an adventure, one usually found me, and now I weave those tales into my stories. I am blessed to have written the bestselling Detective Jack Stratton Mystery-Thriller Series. The collection includes *And Then She Was GONE, Girl Jacked, Jack Knifed, Jacks Are Wild, Jack and the Giant Killer, Data Jack, Jack of Hearts, Jack Frost,* with *Jack of Diamonds* due later this year. I have also penned the bestselling psychological thriller, *The Girl Who Lived* and a special collection of mysteries, *The Adventures of Finn and Annie.*

My background is an eclectic mix of degrees in theatre, communications, and computer science. Currently I reside in Massachusetts with my lovely wife and two fantastic children. My wife, Katherine Greyson, who is my chief content editor, is an author of her own romance series, *Everyone Keeps Secrets.*

My love for tales of mystery and adventure began with my grandfather, a decorated World War I hero. I will never forget being introduced to his friend, a WWI pilot who flew across the skies at the same time as the feared, legendary Red Baron. My love of reading and storytelling eventually led me to write *Pure of Heart,* a young adult fantasy that I released in 2014.

I love to hear from my readers. Please visit ChristopherGreyson.com, where you can become a preferred reader and enjoy additional FREE *Adventures of Finn and Annie,* advanced notifications of book releases and more! Thank you for reading my novels. I hope my stories have brightened your day.

Sincerely,

CPSIA information can be obtained
at www.ICGtesting.com
Printed in the USA
LVHW032359071219
639780LV00008B/223/P